WILD FATE

BOOK FOUR: BLACK CLAW RANCH

CECILIA LANE

A SHIFTING DESTINIES NOVEL

CONTENTS

CHAPTER 1

Alex Carter pushed himself upright from the bar. Blood pounded in his ears. For a single moment, he reconsidered his actions.

Then he twisted back around, wiping the blood from his lip.

"Come on," he taunted, "is that the best you can do? My dead grandmother hits harder than you."

The man's face purpled with anger. His fists tightened as he drew back for the next punch.

Fuck *yes.*

Alex ducked the first, but took the second right in the ribs. He added his own blows to the mix, loving the release he felt every time he connected with flesh. Fury and hatred and remembered hurts boiled inside him and needed to go somewhere.

Together, he and his opponent crashed between onlookers. Some watched with bored disinterest, nursing their bottles and pints. Others whooped and cheered for the bit of action as they circled and lashed out.

A sudden foot between his own feet stumbled Alex backward. An uppercut flung him over a high-top table. The man was instantly there, holding him down with a firm hand.

"You motherfucker," the man gritted out. "Stick your dick elsewhere."

Alex laughed, long and loud and crazed. *Do it,* he silently urged. *End it.*

He didn't even know what prompted the fight. Flirting with the wrong woman, probably. Too much to drink, likely.

Just wanting to fuck some shit up, definitely.

His bear roared in his head, but the noise and desires went unacknowledged. Sharp claws raked up his insides and demanded he paint the bar red with the man's blood.

Wild bear. Insane bear. He needed to be put down.

"The fuck is this?" Gideon Bloodwing yelled over the noise. He shoved through the onlookers and caught the man's fist right before he slammed *could* it into Alex's nose.

Pity.

"Back off," Gideon snapped. He turned to Alex, eyes glowing silver. "Your clan is coming to get you. Wait outside before you start another fight and I have more tables and glasses added to your tab."

"Just adding some entertainment to a boring night, Bloodwing," Alex snarked. He tongued his teeth and spun in a slow circle.

"Third time this week." Gideon glowered. "Out. Now."

The simple thing—the smart thing—would have been to leave. Gideon was a dragon. A literal, fire-breathing murder machine with his own set of issues. The dangerous look flashing in his eyes only needled Alex more.

He picked up the nearest pint and swallowed it down, gesturing for Gideon to make him leave.

Gideon knocked the glass out of his hand and to the floor, shattering shards in all directions. Then he wrapped a firm hand around the back of Alex's neck and shoved him through the crowd. Gideon used Alex's face as a battering ram to throw open the bar door and sent him sprawling into the parking lot.

"Stay out," the dragon growled, smoke curling out of his snarling lips.

Alex raised both his middle fingers in salute. When the door shut with a loud thud, he pushed himself to his feet started toward his truck. Wait for his clan? Nah. He didn't need his alpha's disappointment or anyone else's shit. He had enough of his own to weigh him down.

The outside was too quiet. The dreaded silence itched at the back of his head and let too many unwanted memories bubble to the surface. Fuck, he was sick of those thoughts and the feelings they brought.

His bear rolled through him with the desperate need to shift.

Yeah, fuck that. He'd already done so four times that day alone. Many, many more if he added up the week. A lifetime worth if he counted the month.

Skies above, he hated April.

The night sky wasn't unlike the one from six years ago. Same twinkling stars breaking up the velvety blue-black wrapping around every cursed asshole taking a breath. A world of difference existed between that old version of himself and the one pressing at the fading bruises on his cheek.

Alex's bear growled, overriding all human

attempts to contain the noise. His skin broke out in a cold sweat and the sudden clenching of his stomach nearly doubled him over.

Fuck. *Fuck*, not again. Not now.

Headlights slashed across the parking lot. His vision swam and he couldn't tell if they belonged to someone turning into the bar or leaving the barbecue joint across the street.

He could still feel the teeth of the bear cutting into his arms and legs. Claws tore up his middle, but not well enough to finish the job. He didn't know exactly when he lost consciousness. Sometime after being dragged away from the campsite, for sure. The crinkle of twigs and leaves breaking under his body were as deeply imprinted on his brain as the rest of the sounds and smells of that horrifying night.

With a snarl, he tore off his shirt and gave in to the bear pacing away under his skin.

Cracks and pops ripped through him with blinding pain. No one ever warned about the fast shifts. Slower ones eased into the pain of a body changing from one shape to another. Drew it out, but made it manageable. A man could breathe through those.

The fast and hard ones, supposed signs of a powerful beast, were like tearing off a bandage.

Quick and done, but the pain lingered long after the sudden rip.

The bear's giant paws tingled with sharp jabs of pins and needles as he ran toward the river and into the mountains surrounding Bearden.

He clawed up trees as he passed, gouging them while pretending they were the face and form of their maker. That beast haunted his dreams. A good life was ruined in the span of a bear attack.

The first time he woke—alone, bloodied, and shockingly still alive—his bear shoved him aside and took the driver's seat. Full of rage and hurt, he put his nose to the ground and tried to sniff out the unfamiliar scent of their maker.

Alex hadn't known anything then. Hadn't known about shifters or rogues or what shifters did to rogues caught forcibly changing unsuspecting humans. He'd understood one thing, only.

He was different and dangerous.

Not a damn thing had changed in the years since.

Cracks in the distance. Rustling of branches and leaves. Alex slowed and cocked his head. Someone wanted to sound the alarm on their approach.

Ethan lumbered out of the trees. The bear sized him up immediately. Bigger, but only by a hair. Cool confidence rolled off the other bear, like he understood exactly where he belonged in the world.

Alex and his bear both wanted to tear that place down and set it on fire.

Ethan's fur melted away until a man crouched in the dirt. He picked through the pack that had fallen from his mouth and tugged on a pair of jeans.

"Shift," Ethan ordered.

Alex growled at the power infused in the word. He shook his head to clear the stinging firing through his ears and down his spine. Muscles braced against the command from his alpha.

Ethan leveled him with a steady look. "Shift," he repeated.

The bear again shook his head. Claws pawed at the dirt underfoot. Anger bubbled to the surface that anyone would dare order him around.

Fuck. Shit. Alex panted, locked away inside the bear. Maybe this was it. He'd been poking and prodding for years, slowly getting worse with each anniversary. Every single deathday card he received, coated in a scent he'd never forget, drove him a little closer to the edge of insanity.

The rogue who turned him was a fucking monster. He slipped closer to becoming that same villain each passing day.

Ethan would have to put him down eventually. Alex prayed for a quick death. Ethan was an honorable man; he'd make it fast.

"*Shift*," Ethan ordered for a third time.

Something broke inside the bear and a rush of twisting, snapping pain doused Alex in another cold sweat.

His chest heaved as he sucked in breath after breath and willed his limbs to stop shaking. When he finally found the will to sit up, he found a pair of jeans next to him and Ethan sitting not far away. His alpha pretended to be engrossed in the noises of the night, but the stiff set of his shoulders and the slight tilt of his head said his focus fell on Alex.

Shit. No escaping the bullshit words of wisdom.

He should have broken more chairs and tables at the bar. Maybe a window. Something worthwhile to deserve the unwanted pep talk.

Alex eyed the mountain peaks above him and calculated the time it'd take to run up one and throw himself off. With his luck, Ethan would order him to sit his ass down and listen.

Silent growl in his throat, he shoved himself into his jeans and took a seat far enough from Ethan to make his intrusion known.

Couldn't a man wallow in self-pity and find a fight in peace?

Ethan pulled a bottle from his pack, took a swig, and passed it over. "You made it another year. Happy changing day, fucker."

Alex glared and snatched the bottle. Three huge gulps burned fire down his throat, but didn't touch the raw unease still scratching at him.

"You get another card?"

Alex stared straight ahead and took another gulp. They were the same every year. Birthday cards meant for children, counting up the years since he'd been turned. No address, no signature. Just the rotting, stinking scent that invaded his nose on the day of his death and transition into something else.

"Gideon filled me in on what happened tonight. Said you didn't even talk to that man's girlfriend, but the moment he started popping off, you stepped in. You were looking for a fight, weren't you?"

His bear growled and paced. Fight. A sending whipped through him. The world painted in red. Another fight. More blood. More opportunities to find a quick death and end things before he got too bad.

"You're not the first to have trouble adjusting to this life. I know it wasn't easy on you coming into this without a clue. Might be easier on some now that they know about us, I don't know. They aren't my clan. You are." Ethan leaned over to grab the bottle and took his own sip before handing it back. "I haven't lost one of you yet. I don't plan on letting that happen anytime soon."

Alex shrugged noncommittally. He didn't live in a shifter town without knowing what happened to those who lacked control. They were dangers that needed to be put down. The act was a favor to everyone involved. The crazy asshole was put out of his misery, the good-intentioned alpha was freed of a problem, and the rest of the fucking world was saved from an unpredictable danger.

"Tansey didn't have good control after Viho changed her, either. She could hardly walk the first time she shifted," Ethan said with warm fondness lacing his tone and scent.

Alex lifted his lip at the mention of Tansey. Not at *her*, her, just the idea of her. She was Ethan's mate. Marked, claimed, fated, all the trappings.

He thought he had someone like her once. His maker stole her from him, too.

Hunter had Joss. Lorne had Sloan. Soon enough, even Jesse would have someone regularly licking his dick.

Which left Alex out in the cold.

Another line between him and the others. They had futures. He looked forward to death. They had people surrounding them with bullshit kumbayas and fuzzy feelings. He had memories of pain and cut himself off from everyone he once knew.

Including Liv.

Beautiful Liv. Perfect body, silky hair, creamy skin. Smart as a whip, too. Wild when she wasn't hitting the books and outmatching everyone in her class. And she wanted him. Dumb fuck army brat who just wanted to play in the dirt all day.

Alex killed the memory of the woman. No good would come from dragging up the past.

He was a hollow man and nothing could fill the void. He couldn't go a day without shifting or his inner animal made life unbearable. No amount of drinking or fucking quieted the beast inside him for long.

Ethan started talking again about making plans, getting his bear under control. He made veiled threats of locking Alex down before he spent another night in the drunk tank or drew the attention of zealots in the Supernatural Enforcement Agency.

Alex just stared into the night. He didn't even

have the energy to mouth off. Fuck if that wasn't a sign of the end times. He hated being locked in his head.

He was getting worse, not better. There wasn't any control to be had.

Better if Ethan just put him down before he lost the last bit of sanity and became like the monster that created him.

CHAPTER 2

"Are you sure this is what you want?"

Liv West straightened and closed her eyes for a brief moment to steel herself. Luckily she already had most of her bags packed, so she was ready for the guilt trip.

The stairs to her room creaked as her mother approached, continuing with her running commentary about Liv's life. "I just don't see why you need to go *there*."

"That's where the research facility is, Mom. I can't exactly work there and not be there."

Her mother gave her a flat look as she took a seat on the bed next to the open suitcase. Liv folded another shirt and placed it inside. The fresh laundry pile grew smaller with each item stashed away. Her nerves replaced the mountain of clothing. Once she was done, she was free to leave. She just had one obstacle to get through before she drove off toward her dream job.

"They're dangerous, Liv. I know you want to work on this shifter thing, but are you sure you're going to be safe?"

"Mom," Liv groaned. "This is my decision. It's a great opportunity."

She'd dealt with the thinly veiled disapproval from the moment she'd spilled what her job would entail. Oh, her mother was glad she would help with the 'shifter thing' but she meant it in the 'make them all disappear' sort of way. Anything strange and different didn't have a place in Nancy West's world.

"There are other jobs, Liv. Places closer to home. Closer to your family." Her mother picked up a stuffed bear, a relic from Liv's childhood, and sat it on her lap. Her perfectly done up lips frowned and her voice took on a higher, babyish pitch. "Don't you want a family, Livvy?"

"Yes, Mom. One day," Liv answered. "I'm busy working on myself right now."

The talk wasn't unexpected. Frankly, Liv was impressed she'd avoided it for so long. Her mother had kept her shit together during the weeks of transition, but now it was time.

Liv hated being forced back under her parents' roof. The soft pink walls and floral comforter were meant for a girl still with her innocence and a whole heart. She'd broken out of the shelter her parents tried to keep her in on the day she left for college. Not once in all the years since had she looked back.

But with needing to give up her apartment lease and a delayed start date at her new job, she'd stared down the barrel of either a temporary rental or her childhood bedroom. One cost a fortune in real money, but the other demanded a different currency.

"Your brothers were married by your age."

And there it was. The crux of their issues. Her mother was a homemaker longing for a time when women went to school for their MRS degree and daughters didn't move further than the next block over. That Liv had gotten her Ph.D. instead was a foreign idea. Her brothers, good country boys both, went into business together doing construction work. At the appropriate age, they found wives and popped out a couple kids each.

She loved her brothers and their partners and the nieces and nephews that seemed to sprout several inches every time she saw them, but that life wasn't for her. Not anymore.

"I know. I was there." What was the saying? Always the bridesmaid and never the bride. Yeah, that was her future.

"Luke, he was a nice boy. You had fun with him," her mother continued. "And Nicholas. Oh, Nicholas was such a sweetheart last Christmas. What happened to him?"

Liv kept her focus on the laundry pile. "He moved back to the other coast."

"And what was wrong with him? You could have gone with him."

Liv imagined a stone under running water. Smooth, unbothered by anything above the surface. She needed to be that stone, or the interrogation wouldn't ever end. "We just weren't that compatible."

"You don't give them a chance," Nancy scoffed with a dismissive wave of her hand. "I just think you put too much of yourself into school and work. Where's the fun in that, Livvy? You have to stop and smell the roses sometimes."

"I had fun, Mom. Remember when you had to send me bail money after getting caught with booze in the dorm?" she reminded. Oh, undergrad had some days of drinking and partying. She just left those a little early and hit the books, or made sure she fit in the fun between classes.

"What was that boy's name?"

Liv froze. Fuck. She shouldn't have touched on those years.

"Alex. Yes, that's it." Her mother's eyes brightened as the light bulb went off. "Alex was the trouble-maker who got you arrested. What a wicked little punk. I was glad when he showed his true colors and gave you a chance to move on."

Alex. Fucking Alex. Just the mention of his name drove a knife through her heart. She wanted to be furious with him, but he only brought her pain.

Well, not just her. All the men who came after him, too. Those nice boys, the sweet boys, the pleasant talkers. The ones her mother approved of. They were nothing compared to Alex. They didn't have his fire. They were safe.

Which was why they never lasted long.

Asshole. That was Alex. The asshole who up and left her while she was away at a conference, then rubbed her face in it whenever their paths crossed those last weeks on campus. She was grateful he didn't tear their group of friends apart, but that was because he dropped them, too.

"We're not discussing this anymore," Liv snapped.

She didn't bother folding the rest of her clothes and dumped them into her suitcase. The rips of the zipper cut off the rest of her mother's arguments.

She put up with comparisons to her brothers and their perfect families. She could deal with reminders of failed relationships. But Alex was a subject Liv couldn't rehash.

She just wanted acceptance and a hint of understanding. She thought she had it. Once. Many years and miles of heartbreak ago. She didn't need to feel those same nauseating disappointments stemming from her own mother.

"Livvy," her mother pouted.

"I really need to get going. Daylight's wasting," she said. The suitcase hit the carpet with a dull thunk and she dragged it out the door.

Her mother followed her down the steps. "There's still time to change your mind. You can stay here as long as you like. Your brothers miss you. You've hardly spent time with their kids."

"Mom, I'm doing this," Liv said firmly.

She glanced around the foyer one last time. She'd desperately wanted out of the house as a teen. That same scratching urge to leave had clung to her when she moved back in for a few short weeks. But now that the final moment had arrived, sadness for the life she could have had welled in her stomach.

No home to call her own. No partner to meet her exasperated look when her mother did something overbearing for the thousandth time. No kids stomping up and down the stairs.

Alex took so much when he left.

Quiet buzzed in the room and Liv turned to find her mother watching her with big, sad eyes.

They were the only ones in the house. The big family gathering and gauntlet of goodbyes had been the night before.

One more hug, then she could get on the road.

Her mother wrapped her up tight. After a stiff second, Liv melted into the embrace.

"I feel like I'm dropping you off at college all over again," Nancy murmured thickly. She dabbed at her eyes when she pulled away. "Maybe you'll meet someone there who will make you happy."

Moment ruined.

"Sure, Mom. There's always hope." Liv kept the sarcasm out of her voice.

Alex taught her a valuable lesson.

Better to be alone than to hurt.

CHAPTER 3

Liv drove through the small town of Bearden, balancing her fresh cup of coffee with the meandering bends in the road. The main strip disappeared in her rearview and left her with the bright greens and crisp scent of spring in the mountains as she drove toward the Bearden Research Facility.

Nerves piled up in her stomach and churned with her second injection of caffeine that morning. The first had been needed to wake her up from a restless night of new job jitters. The second was her morning routine and an easy way to scope out the early morning happenings of Bearden.

The town moved slowly, which was a change of pace. One she appreciated after years of living and working in a big city. The people were friendlier, too, and willing to offer greetings instead of ducking their eyes during shared commutes.

One day in the town, and she was already enamored. The food choices left a lot to be desired with the simple lack of variety, but the barbecue and coffee places—her only samples so far—made up for it with delicious food and treats.

And of course, there was that 'shifter thing.'

Her mother had texted her at least eight dozen times since Liv arrived at the rental set aside for research workers. She'd wanted to know the moment Liv first encountered one of those dangerous creatures, but Liv disappointed her when she described a quick check-in and food delivery.

Truth be told, she was a little disappointed herself. Her mother's griping almost had her expecting wilderness and wild animals roaming the streets. Not a single shifter or vampire knocked at her door.

The final test of seeing if she could cut it in Bearden was stepping into her new position.

Liv flicked on the blinker and made the turn into the facility parking lot.

She frowned at the small crowd in front of the building. She'd been warned about them, but didn't put much thought into their existence until then.

Protesters from both sides of the aisle glared at one another and hoisted signs in the air. The human contingent of about ten men and women expressed their displeasure at other humans sullying themselves by working on the supernatural problem. The supernatural side was made up of six shifters angry —and no doubt afraid—that any research into them would bring about their destruction.

Liv pushed out of her car and shouldered her purse. Barricades kept the protestors from blocking the entrance, but they did nothing to mask the dark and sullen looks lobbed from one side to the other. The bored guard standing at the door looked even less useful.

She took a deep breath. No use waiting around. She strode through the parking lot and straight for the front doors of the Bearden Research Facility.

Murmurs greeted her ears once both groups realized where she headed. "Traitor!" someone shouted.

Liv turned to the voice and blinked at the sudden flash of a camera.

"This way, ma'am," the guard said before she could react. He stepped aside and held open the door to the lobby.

Another guard stood next to a metal detector and a table with small trays for personal items. Liv calmly jotted down her name since she still needed to be issued proper identification and passed through the machine. No unwanted beeps or alarms sounded, but she looked back over her shoulder. Two guards and some flimsy barricades didn't seem like much protection if those outside wanted to get in.

Then the guard touched fingers to his hat and slid her purse to her. Under the brim, his eyes glowed.

Shifter.

She definitely wasn't in Kansas anymore.

A petite blonde woman practically bounced on her toes on the other side of the security station. As soon as Liv picked up her purse, the woman rushed forward with her hand outstretched. "Dr. Olivia West? It's a pleasure to finally meet you in person."

"Liv, please," she said, shaking her hand. "Olivia was my grandmother."

"Oh, and I'm Rylee. Strathorn." A wide smile graced her lips before she shut it down for a more professional demeanor. "Director of the facility here."

Liv pointed over her shoulder. "Are they supposed to take pictures?"

"Oh, them." Rylee frowned. "Happens to all the

newbies. Because a little photo shoot is supposed to be scarier than waking up to a one-ton bear shifter on your front porch. Ignore them, and welcome to Bearden. Our monsters beat up their monsters."

Before Liv could respond, Rylee bustled into another ramble. "Not that we're monsters, of course! We have teams working on every facet of knowledge to be gained here in Bearden. We want to understand just how the supernatural citizens came to be here and if there really is a veil between our world and their original one. Historical, anthropological, and linguistic teams are studying the various creation myths connected to the enclaves. There's great interest in the study of the Broken, too, and just how their magic can power a barrier to hide the entire enclave.

"You'll be working on the serum team, of course. Those labs are on the second floor." Rylee adjusted her glasses. "They're near and dear to my own heart, so you get the tour from me. Aren't you lucky."

Liv chuckled. The woman was a delight after so many years under stuffy scientists without an ounce of social grace. She already felt at ease. "Lead the way."

Rylee shot off toward the elevators and jabbed a button to summon one. "It's mostly sample collection at this point. We have a couple experiments running, but nothing close to the results we're looking for. To be expected, of course. It took Dr. Edward Jenner years of work and research before the smallpox vaccine procedure was truly understood. Then a couple hundred more to perfect the current form. Our research is really in its infancy, but that's why I'm collecting the most brilliant minds to work for me."

"I'm honored to be here," Liv said.

No lie, either. Meeting Dr. Rylee Strathorn herself was an honor, let alone to be welcomed into the facility. Liv had been glued to the television during the public hearings when shifters and other supernaturals like vampires and fae were first revealed to the world. Rylee fought hard for the town of Bearden and her vision of future research. Quiet, sometimes rambling, she had a firm manner when needed. Liv was excited to get a personal introduction from the woman.

"Good. Very good. I expect hard work out of everyone." The elevator doors opened, and they stepped inside. "Have you had much contact with shifters before this?"

"None," Liv answered. The doors shuttered away

the lobby and started to move. "Though I'm sure I've met some and just didn't know it."

"Rule of thumb around town is to assume you're not dealing with a human. We're the minority here. Sharp ears and sharp eyes, remember that."

The elevator dinged open and they stepped into a long hallway with many doors, most guarded by a keypad and card reader. Rylee paused at a set of doors near the end of the hall and swiped her card in the lock. She swung the door wide open with a grand gesture. "Here we are."

Liv stepped through and felt exactly like Belle finding the Beast's library. Lab stations ran around the room. Microscopes and centrifuges rested between computers and other equipment. Large refrigerators no doubt held all the samples collected and used for the experiments currently running.

"State of the art everything," Rylee said as she led her through the lab. "We fight hard for our budget. And right through here will be your desk."

Through another set of doors was an open office. Desks were grouped together facing each other and lined up in rows with walking space between each set. Small dividers separated each space, but not enough to give any true sense of privacy. They were expected to collaborate, Liv knew. The team had no room for egos.

A few of the desks were occupied, and those seated shot her warm smiles as Rylee led her to one at the very end.

"I know you've probably already heard the spiel about our end goals here, but I'll add my own," Rylee started. "Some of the cases we've come across—volunteers or thrown our way by the Supernatural Enforcement Agency—would break your heart. I've helped place a father bitten on a camping trip with the pack in Wolfden, but prior to this, he'd have been completely on his own. He's still dealing with the lifestyle changes, of course. Lots of rare steaks and walking on the furry side in his future.

"He's one of the lucky ones. He has a solid support system around him. The ones I really want to help are the poor souls who wouldn't have a chance of survival." Her face fell and she shook her head. "For whatever reason, some just reject the changes to their makeup. I've tried gathering numbers, but secret societies weren't exactly big on record keeping. What I *can* conclude is women tend to have better odds than men, but turning into a shifter still risks death. Those are the people I want to give a chance. That's why we're trying to find a way to reverse the changes."

Rylee's passion was exactly what drew Liv to the program. When the first recruiter approached her about confidential work, she'd assumed something involving the military. Her second interview laid the groundwork for dealing with the supernatural.

Confronted with her own desk and the actual lab, the nerves that plagued her before slipped into nothing. She was happy to have made it through the hoops to wind up in the lab. "So where do I begin?"

Rylee fished in her pocket and pulled out a set of keys. She bent and unlocked the file cabinet nestled at the end of a desk row. The drawer rolled out and revealed a number of charts inside.

"Here. We have several program volunteers living in Bearden. They come in monthly, we ask our questions, they give us their samples, and we make an appointment for the next month. Others here are coordinating with satellite offices in other enclaves, but you'll be working directly with our Bearden residents. Familiarize yourself with their files. I'm sure once Dr. Franco, our lab manager, returns from a satellite office, he'll shadow you for the initial follow-ups. Some of our volunteers can be a bit testy about changes. Once you're settled, he'll walk you through the trials. Welcome to the team, Liv."

When Rylee left, the rest of the lab assistants swarmed. Liv tried to remember all the names. Jenny Barnes was her desk partner, so she was easy to remember. Barry O'Shea, Chuck Wilson, Leela Biswas, Robbie Peters, Matt Simmons... The frantic meet-and-greet ended with lots of handshakes, directions to the coffee machine, and promises to let them show her around town.

When the room settled back into routine, Liv pulled charts from the first three letters of the alphabet. Of the A through Cs, there were about fifteen charts to go through. Liv took a seat at her desk and opened the first one.

Photos were stapled to the front of the paperwork. Digging into the details, Liv saw most were changed by shifters they knew. The timing was varied, too, with some no earlier than a few weeks to those who'd spent decades with an animal under their skin. Blood, hair, and saliva samples were collected and dates noted. The final document asked for consent for potential future trials to reverse the changes, but only one in the B group had checked the box.

Liv opened the second file in the C pile and

gasped. Her stomach tightened with a sick, oily sensation of upset and loss.

Alex looked back at her.

Liv stared, hard, then looked over her shoulder. No one else in the room paid her any attention. No practical jokers took an initiation much, much too far.

Six years, and all the unresolved hurt came rushing back.

There had been a time when she thought they would marry and have the pack of grandchildren her mother wanted. In fact, Liv was certain the camping trip he planned to take while she was away at a conference was him and his friends having one last hoorah before he proposed.

Walking off her plane to find no one waiting for her was a shock. Finding their apartment emptied broke her completely. He'd ripped the rug out from under her with a one-two punch of abandonment and betrayal.

Holy fuck. To see him again after so long... She didn't know what to think or feel.

Her brain slowly rebooted and her eyebrows shot together.

The program only dealt with bitten shifters. That she held his file in her hands meant he wasn't born into a supernatural family. Which made sense; she couldn't imagine his stern father ever allowing for any animalistic nonsense.

Feeling guilty, Liv peeked under Alex's photo and checked the details. A deep pit filled her middle when she scanned over the date of his change.

Six years. The month and year slapped her in the face.

Liv pushed back on the wave of hurt she felt anytime she let herself recall those last weeks of grad school. That date was the answer he refused to give her, the final reason he'd left her so suddenly and without a word.

Alex was a bear shifter.

Liv chewed her lip. Ethically, was she okay? Physically, mentally, emotionally, those were all too far away for her to process. The job required an answer.

She'd have to discuss it with the lab manager, and maybe go all the way up to Dr. Strathorn. Like any other lab she'd worked in, there was probably a process to separate people who couldn't get along. Sample collection wasn't anything big or important. Someone else could always deal with Alex directly.

Everything else welled up with the possible resolution. Her heart pounded as she studied his photo.

He'd aged in the six years since she last saw him. His easy smile had turned into a hard scowl, too. His hair was a mess, his cheeks stubbled, and he didn't quite look at the camera.

Time and experience hadn't been kind to him.

Part of her wanted to snark 'good!' and pour herself a stiff drink. The smaller, deeply hidden part that still remembered him fondly wanted to understand.

Lifestyle changes, Rylee mentioned. Some didn't make it out alive. Others were so violent and troubled, they were forced to cut their years short with a quick death.

Alex had been changed before shifters were out in the open. Maybe there was a reason for him turning into a giant asshole.

Liv steeled herself against the sorrow and leaned on her anger. Whatever had happened, she wasn't about to give up the opportunity of a lifetime. She wasn't going to quit her job because he was involved in a related project. Their paths would cross eventually. She could be an adult about the situation. She expected him to behave like one, too. She'd extend him a courtesy and let him know she was in town.

Liv jotted down the address listed in his file and stuffed it into her purse.

CHAPTER 4

L iv slowed and eyed the sign on the side of the road, then glanced at the map on her phone. The little dot of location bounced around and the route constantly shifted, changed, and refused to confirm if she was, indeed, at the right place to find Black Claw Ranch.

Trusting the sign, she passed over the bumpy cattle grate and inched up the winding path. Deep ruts threatened to strand her little car. She understood why her brothers preferred their big trucks she'd needed to climb into.

On the crest of a small hill, she got her first look at the place. Two big buildings lorded over the space between them, one clearly meant for living and the other for the practical nature of ranch work. The main house was an oversized log cabin with two floors and a couple decks on the upper level jutting out for private viewing of the land. The main level was lined by a long porch with wooden columns.

The barn was unpainted, with both doors thrown open. Two trucks were parked near it, but she didn't spot anyone outside. A single horse grazing in the nearby fenced area was the only creature in sight.

Liv pulled to a stop next to the trucks and stepped outside after another curious glance. This was where Alex ended up. The place wasn't entirely surprising. He'd always been interested in the outdoors. He'd turned the interest into a job as a ranch hand, it seemed. The gig suited her memory of him.

She poked her head into the barn and smiled at the horses that stuck their heads over the stall doors. But they didn't offer her any of the answers she needed, so she stepped around to the edge of the building to peek on the other side.

A small calf lazed in the sun, looking quite content despite the trash talk coming from the man standing nearby.

"*Now* it's time to sleep?" he grumbled. "Not during the actual night, but now, while the sun is still out? I hope you get nice and fat with all this lounging around you do. You'll make a better steak."

Alex. She'd recognize his voice anywhere.

He chewed on a piece of hay, long strand stuck between lips she knew the taste of. The sun glistened off his skin like he'd been rubbed down in oil and posed perfectly for a camera. Over his heart was a rough symbol tattooed in a teenage rebellion over moving from Okinawa and back to the States. He'd added new ink, she noted, blossoms mixed in wind or waves, she wasn't sure which.

His hair clung to his head, a few strands curling in stubborn protest at being swept back with the hand he passed over them. The cut looked rough and choppy, like he'd taken scissors to it himself.

Then there were the horrid scars running up and down his arms. Faint like they were old, but unnaturally shiny, they were the mark of a bitten shifter. They didn't tell a story of a peaceful change.

Liv thought she'd gotten a handle on herself when she first saw his picture, but that idea flew out the window when confronted with the living, breathing, real thing.

Six years, and everything flooded back.

Her stomach immediately started to flutter and other bits of her warmed. That was the problem with Alex. They were extremely compatible in certain areas and direct opposites in others. Like relationships, lying, and running off without a word.

But damn did he give her an amazing time in bed.

Alex turned and Liv froze.

Human green eyes brightened unnaturally and stopped her in her tracks.

Holy hell, they were glowing.

"What are you doing here, Liv?" he asked in a defeated tone that cut her deep.

She straightened her shoulders. Better get on with it, then. "I didn't want there to be any surprises or awkwardness if you saw me on the street or at work. I'm working in the labs. I saw your chart."

"You're working—" He cut himself off with a scowl. "You know what, take me off the lists. Get out of here. Don't call me, don't visit. Turn around and walk away if you see me in town."

"That's it?" An incredulous laugh puffed past her lips. Well, the encounter was spinning out of control and far beyond the scope she intended. "After everything, you just blow me off?"

"What more is there to say? I'm leaving the program. There's nothing else to discuss."

"Nothing else? You don't think you owe me an

explanation?"

"I don't owe you anything." Alex pointed behind her. "Road's that way."

Liv tried to bite her tongue and failed. The utter dismissal in his voice drove her up a wall. She'd put up with a lack of answers, she'd lived with the loneliness, she'd kept putting one foot in front of the other. But deep down, he still took up too much space in her head.

"You broke up with me in a text message!" Anger and hurt flushed over her cheeks. "And that was after I got home to find all your stuff gone. I didn't know if you were in an accident or if something happened, then you drop that bomb on me. And if that wasn't bad enough, anytime we were in the same room, you were shoving your tongue down the throat of any girl with a pulse!" Liv ground her teeth together and glared at him. "So yeah, I think I'm owed an explanation."

Alex shrugged and tossed her an infuriating smile. "Sounds like a you problem." *have? had*

How? How could any one person be such an asshole? "You haven't changed a damn bit since the last time I saw you," she spat.

"Last time is key. You shouldn't have come here."

"Forgive me for wanting to give you a heads up.

39

I'm not one to spring things on someone unexpectedly."

He didn't answer her. Instead, he bent to retrieve the shirt at his feet and strode for the barn.

Oh, hell no. He did not get to walk away from her. He'd gotten away with it before, but that was a different time. A different place. She'd been too hurt to pursue her answers then, but she was stronger than ever and ready to confront him.

She desperately wanted to be over him. He was six years gone and left a trail of failed relationships in his wake. He was at the center of it all. She couldn't imagine feeling as strongly for someone ever again. She didn't want the hurt that came when they left.

And under all that, she was *pissed*. At him then, at him now.

She zipped around the side of the barn and stormed right through the doors to see him slipping in through a stall. He scowled in her direction and turned to walk away from her again, but she followed on his heels.

"I thought you could be grown up enough to work in close quarters," she sniped, "but I can see you're still just the same coward that runs away instead of owning up to a damn thing."

Alex growled at whatever fresh hell he'd been dragged into. Six years, and there she was. Taller than most girls, hips and legs for days, swell of her fucking perfect tits not at all hidden under her conservative top.

Six years, and he couldn't get away.

He knew he shouldn't give in to the trap she set with her words, but she'd strung a ring through his nose the first time he saw her. Now here she was, still yanking him around.

"Coward?" he bristled. He spun to face her. Fucking hell, he needed to get away from her. "I'm not a coward."

What could he tell her? That he'd been afraid for her life? He'd left to protect her? Those kisses and other girls she talked about were just pawns. Warm bodies to soothe the gnawing hunger inside him, a hunger that existed solely for her. They meant nothing, were nothing, still made him feel nothing. No one could hold a candle to her.

But they were all he had when he couldn't trust himself with her.

He'd been born into a world that didn't exist. He hadn't known how to navigate the changes and urges and fucking ton of hard packed, muscled murder machine that he turned into whenever he got too pissed. And fuck, was he still pissed. The monster that changed him stole his fucking life.

Stole *her*.

How could he tell her that he missed her every fucking second of the day and still keep her away? Those days of easy laughs and weekends spent in bed were long gone.

Black hair rustled with the force of her denial. Shorter than ever, but he imagined those strands were still silky smooth. The angled cut suited her. Made her look fierce.

"I just don't see the need to rehash what happened," he added before she could speak. "Go find some ice cream and cry it out with someone else."

A storm of anger swirled in her narrowed, grey eyes. Red splotched her cheeks and made her look even sexier.

He twisted away and ignored the press of his bear to run his nose against her skin and lick her from head to toe.

"I know what you are," she said between gritted teeth.

Alex whipped around. His hands landed on her

waist and he backed her up against a wall faster than she could expel the air from her lungs.

"You know what I am? And what is that, Liv?" He skimmed his nose up her neck and swallowed down her delicious scent. Coconut and flowers, if he remembered all the bottles of shampoos and body washes that littered their shower correctly.

And of course, he fucking remembered. No detail went unturned over the years.

Fuck, he'd smelled her even before he turned and saw her. Jaw-droppingly gorgeous, as always. And for once, instead of mauling him from the inside out, his bear just went silent.

Alex nipped her earlobe. "What do you think you know about me?"

"Shifter. That's it, right? That's why you pushed me away?" She lifted her chin and tried to stare into his eyes.

Tough woman. Smart as hell. She'd fought to be treated with respect by some of her bad-mannered colleagues who didn't know how to interact with a woman. Now she stared him down with a demand in her gaze.

"You don't know a damn thing." He obliterated her objection with a harsh kiss.

Sweet fuck. Her skin felt hot under his palms.

More than anger clogged up his nose, too. Thick, creamy, delicious arousal grabbed him by the balls and rushed blood straight to his dick. Too many clothes separated them, but that didn't stop him from rolling his hips against her or grinning at the resulting choked groan.

She molded to him perfectly, tucked against all the right places, skin and body soft and sweet. He wanted more than a kiss. He wanted her.

Fuck, it'd been the same from the start. The need to possess her only sharpened after his ordeal.

His bear surged forward then, making his presence and desires known.

Bite. Mark. Claim.

Same as when he'd stepped foot into their apartment after everything. She was gone for some presentation, but her scent coated every surface and clung to the sheets. The beast had gone wild inside him, ripping him apart in the urge to get close to her. That was the moment he knew he couldn't stay. He couldn't be trusted to be near her when he had a creature under his skin wanting to sink his teeth in her.

Images swirled in his head. Terrifying ones. Ones with blood on her skin and rips in her flesh, all caused by him. The others, they had their mates and their perfect fucking lives. They didn't have monsters in their middles, always wanting to fight and destroy. Liv would be just another bit of evidence that Ethan should have put him down on day one.

Alex pulled himself away and stepped back, slashing his eyes away from her. He couldn't meet her look. Couldn't see the hurt he put there. Not again. Not ever again.

"There. No awkwardness," he said with a hurtful smirk. "Thanks for stopping by. See you around, maybe."

His bear snarled and slashed at him.

One step. Another. He needed out of the barn and away from her intoxicating scent. Needed to lock himself away before he shifted and tore into her.

Fuck. Fuck.

He forced himself to keep moving, to not turn around. Doing so would bring him to his knees.

Alex stuffed the pain down deep and smothered it with a pillow.

"Asshole," Liv muttered.

He pinned the word to his heart. Yeah, he was an asshole. Better that than letting her close where he could hurt her all over again.

CHAPTER 5

Liv leaned back in her seat and rubbed a hand over her stomach. "That was the best meal I've ever had."

"Oh, I know. If it weren't for all the running around in the lab and during my time off, I'd have gained a thousand pounds by now," Jenny agreed. Others on the serum team nodded up and down the table.

It was the end of their week, and they'd invited Liv to their gathering to unwind. The festivities began at Hogshead Joint for delicious barbecue with plans for drinks at a bar after. She was glad for the chance to get to know them better and pick their brains about the inner workings of small-town life.

Jenny planted her hands on the table. "Anyone up for a drink?"

Leela groaned and shook her head. "You still trying to find yourself a shifter?"

"Desperation isn't a good look," Matt teased.

Jenny shrugged up a shoulder and beamed a look of innocence. "I call it field research."

"I call it tarting it up all over town," Robbie snorted into his pint glass.

The table—Jenny included—burst into laughter. "Sounds like," she gulped back another giggle, "sounds like someone is jealous he's not getting any action."

Robbie raised his hands and conceded the point. "What can I say? It's been a long three months since David's last visit."

"Ah, long distance?" Liv asked.

"He has tenure. This was a great opportunity." Robbie spread his hands again. "Who else can say they're working on the bleeding edge of genetics in another intelligent species?"

Leela nodded. "My parents live on the other side of the world. We video chat once a week, but it's still been a massive change coming here. They get worried whenever they read articles about crimes by or against the supernaturals, as if every single incident is taking place outside my front door. I thought my father was going to come chaperone me everywhere when I was hired."

"Worth it," Chuck added. "Besides, it's like one giant family here once they get to know you. Which is how everyone knows to avoid Jenny like the plague!"

The round of laughter turned to a small roar when Jenny flicked them all off.

Liv sank into the feeling of companionship. Every person she met at the research facility talked with so much passion for their projects. Even the handful of people yelling about their agendas outside couldn't diminish their enthusiasm for the work they did. That she'd been welcomed into the fold was a satisfying relief.

With their bills paid, the group gathered at the edge of the street and prepared to cross.

Jenny spun and walked backward, sly know-it-all look on her face. "It's called The Roost. Best place in town to get a drink, but more than that, a name of significance. Dragons call their little groups clans, like bears, but they also name their homes roosts."

Liv sucked up the knowledge. True or not, she wanted to learn it all.

The group passed through the doors and entered

a crowd inside. Loud country music blared over hidden speakers while a handful of couples swished their hips and spun each other around on the dance floor. Pool tables and two dart boards captured the attention of their own smaller crowds, and the players and watchers cheered, jeered, and swallowed down their drinks.

"He looks busy," Liv said, jerking her chin toward the man behind the bar.

"Gideon Bloodwing. He's a dragon shifter," Jenny whispered. "Fire, scales, wings, the whole shebang. And the owner of the bar."

"And Jenny's next target," Barry added.

They found an open table. The guys let the girls claim the seats, but all leaned in close and continued to tease Jenny or point out someone else in the crowd. By the time their drinks arrived, Liv had a swirl of names and recommendations for how to spend her weekend. Hiking and nature walks were a big draw with the town seated in the mountains. The river held a host of possibilities, too. With the weather warming up, prime spots along the lake would go fast in the morning and stay filled long into the night.

"One of the ranches offers trail rides, too," Chuck mentioned. "I think they're here tonight, actually."

Liv glanced up at that tidbit of information, then looked where he nodded. One man made his way toward an empty seat at the bar.

Alex. And damn, if he didn't look just as good with all his clothes on.

Liv ran her fingers over her lips. Him living in Bearden wasn't anything she expected. Even more surprising had been that kiss he laid on her before walking away.

He jabbed an elbow into the side of one man and twisted away before he could take a punch in return. The group of five sat at the far end of the bar and split their attention between each other and the game playing on a television above the bar.

Strange. Utterly and totally strange to see him after the years they'd shared together and the ones spent apart. Her heart warred with her head. Hurt and anger and curiosity sparked and mixed together. The hows and whys applied to every step that pulled them apart and put them back in each other's orbit.

If she were a believer, she'd say fate played a game with them.

"Excuse me a moment," Liv said to the group and dropped to the floor.

She pushed up to the bar at the opposite end from Alex and his group and ordered three shots of tequila. While waiting, the hair on the back of her neck lifted. She didn't need the quick glance to the side to know she'd been spotted.

Well, so what? She had the beginnings of a plan. She could be the bigger person. She hadn't meant to let him get her hot under the collar.

Hell, the fire from that kiss still burned through her veins.

As did the upset anger of him just walking away like he didn't give a shit about what they'd just done.

Still. She didn't want to flame out a candidate during her first week on the job.

Nor did she want to pretend she didn't know the man.

Liv swallowed one shot and slid the empty back across the bar. She needed liquid courage to combat the swirling mess Alex made of her head.

She sidled up next to him and deposited the shot glasses on the bar. "Alex."

"Liv." Bright green eyes dipped to the glass she nudged closer to him. "What's that?"

"A peace offering. We've found ourselves crossing paths once again. I wanted to apologize for what happened the other day. I hope we can still work together."

"Drink accepted. Apology noted. Scurry back to where you came from." His eyes traveled from the glass and up her body, lingering ever so slightly on her chest before he switched his attention back to the game.

"Not happening." She blocked his hand reaching for the shot glass and slid it closer to hers. Immediately, narrowed eyes returned to her face. "I don't want you quitting because of me. We don't even need to see each other at the lab."

The blond man next to him leaned back. "What's that about a lab?"

Down the line, heads turned and attention swiveled to them. Fuck.

"You're working with them?" another asked.

The one at the end of the row shifted his gaze from her to Alex. "You want to get rid of your bear?" he asked quietly. "That's what they're doing, ain't it? Tansey got asked after she was changed."

Double fuck.

Shifters. She'd been warned about their better senses. And like an idiot, she didn't keep her voice quiet enough.

Alex slammed both shots in quick succession and scowled at the others. "Don't tell me you've never had trouble with your bears."

"Yeah, but it's part of me," the first one answered. "I wouldn't cut off my arm because I broke a finger."

Alex growled, the sound like a pissed off animal warning away anyone who got too close. Liv jerked back, but none of the others reacted.

He shoved to his feet, fixed her with a disgusted look, and made his way for the door. Everyone in his path hurried out of his way.

Liv ignored the questions the others peppered her with and pushed after Alex. She'd really stuck her foot in it this time.

She burst out of the bar door and glanced in every direction. There. He made his way toward a big black truck.

"Alex, wait."

He glanced at her with another disgruntled look and picked up his pace.

"Asshole," she muttered. Louder, she called again, "Alex, stop. I'm sorry."

Alex spun around, glowing green eyes locking with hers. His features twisted up in a savage snarl as he marched in her direction. Liv's heart pounded. He pulled to a stop scary close and poked her hard in the shoulder.

"Fuck off, Liv," he growled. "You think I wanted them to know any of that?"

"I didn't mean for them to overhear," she defended.

"You've ruined enough of my life. Leave me alone."

Liv planted her hands on her hips, all sincere apology forgotten in the remembered hurt that whipped through her. "*I* ruined your life? Oh, that's rich."

Footsteps crossed the parking lot. "Alex, man, hold up. You don't need to rush off."

He shot a withering look to the man behind him. "Don't need to talk it over, Ethan. Just going to check on Daisy and call it a night."

"Daisy?" Liv asked.

Girl's name. Familiar girl's name. One Ethan didn't question.

Liv took a step back and pressed her fingers to her lips. Lips Alex had kissed. "You have a girlfriend?"

Ethan snorted. "He has a—"

"Not your concern, Olivia," Alex snapped over Ethan.

"Wow, Alex." Liv let out a harsh breath. Damn him and the hurt he could still drive into her. She wasn't some naive teenager who thought they'd get married after a single kiss. But grown adults who could stand to be around one another for three seconds? Yeah, she'd hoped for that. Wrongly, it seemed. He'd kissed her with someone else in his life. "Fuck you. You really haven't changed a damn bit. Go home to Daisy."

"Thanks for your permission," he said, voice as full of sarcasm as the little bow and hand wave he gave before turning his back on her again.

Asshole.

Asshole who didn't owe her anything, she reminded herself.

Miserable man. Selfish. Idiot.

Okay, the last was meant for them both. She'd been so stupid to chase after him and expect to get answers. He made it perfectly clear years ago he was happy to blow up their lives without an explanation. Despite her chosen profession, she had to accept that sometimes mysteries stayed unsolved.

Liv turned back to the bar as a truck engine turned over.

CHAPTER 6

Alex pressed his forehead against the kitchen door. He stroked his fingers over the cold doorknob, but couldn't force himself to turn the thing.

Grating, cloying laughter reached his ears and made his bear snarl. Happiness existed on the other side of that door. Full lives. Ones that didn't have everything good torn away and ripped apart.

Damn Liv. Damn her for existing anywhere near him. For having a fantastic fucking life. She'd gone far in her career to snag a job at the research facility. And he was what, wasting away on a ranch and waiting for his alpha to put him down?

His bear slashed at his insides and pressed hard against his control. The beast wanted out.

Too damn bad. His muscles ached and his eyes burned from a lack of sleep. There'd been no bed or dreams when his bear forced a shift on him the moment he threw his truck into park.

Another peal of laughter drove spikes through his eardrums. Not his life. Not his future. He had nothing but pain and madness.

Alex ground his teeth together and bathed himself in irritation. Fuck their joy. This was his job, dammit. He wouldn't let his inner beast push him aside or make him cower. Every inch of him hurt worse than the circumstances of his shifter nature. No sleep, shitty mood. He preferred crawling into a hole to facing his clan.

He ripped open the door and stepped inside.

His muscles protested the fury-driven deter-mination.

The noise—nails on a chalkboard—ceased entirely as soon as the door slammed shut behind him. One by one, faces looked up and stared at him. Joss froze with a spoon halfway to her mouth. Cereal slipped off the side and fell with a splash back into her bowl.

Still eyeing him, Hunter grabbed Joss's hand and licked away a drop of milk. Her giggle broke the stillness of the room.

"What the hell happened last night?" Jesse demanded.

"Ran out of there like your tampon string was on fire," Hunter added.

"Rude," Joss admonished. She wiped her hand down Hunter's arm.

Alex ignored them all. He stomped his way to the coffee maker and poured himself a mug. One breath, then another, and he turned back to the table.

Ethan and Tansey exchanged a look. Volumes were said in that quick gaze.

The royal fucking family. With barely a flick of their eyes, the rest of them fell quiet again, and the inquisition began.

"You're working with the research facility?" Ethan asked.

Tansey nodded, eyes serious for once. "They were interested in me because I was bitten, just like you."

A growl rumbled in Alex's chest and he shook his head. "Not like me," he said in a low voice. She could fuck right off with the comparisons. Tansey had a mate from the start. She had help. She knew what the fuck happened to her.

"Enough that they wanted me to volunteer to give up that part of myself if their program worked."

Tansey didn't shift her focus anywhere. Steady gaze, steady voice. A true match to the alpha at her side.

Fuck, all of them were perfect reflections. Joss and Hunter were stupidly in love. Sloan and Lorne held each other together.

He wouldn't have that pairing. He'd burned that support to the ground.

His bear dug claws into his brain and burned through his veins.

"I gave you a space here," Ethan said, soft words hiding the knife of disappointment underneath. "Somewhere safe to help—"

"Yeah, well, didn't help as much as any of us wanted," Alex growled.

"There's no reason to rush into anything. I know this month is difficult—"

"Difficult?" Alex laughed harshly. Silver sparked in Ethan's eyes as a warning he promptly ignored. "Difficult is getting stuck in traffic. This is a reminder of how everything went wrong."

"Haven't you been doing okay?" Sloan asked softly.

"Asking so you know if you need to put in a kill order for me with your psycho cop friends?" If it wasn't Ethan to put him down, it'd be the damn SEA with their place at the breakfast table courtesy of Lorne and his agent mate.

"Ease up," Lorne snapped. His fingers pressed into the table and his eyes blazed at the insult to his mate. "No one is reporting anyone. We're just trying to get some answers."

"We doing things by committee now? Everyone taking a vote on me?" He pointed at Lorne. "You know what it's like to feel death breathing down your neck." To Hunter. "To feel utterly out of control." Jesse and Ethan. "Knowing you can't go back to the way things were. None of you have the slightest idea what I feel every time I wake up. That clawing, throbbing, insistent need to run and fight. I want to bleed every one of you every second of the day."

There. The words were out in the open.

He wanted blood and fur. He wanted to fight. He'd been made in an act of murder and brawling was the only thing that soothed the beast under his skin.

Ethan blinked slowly. Deliberately. Like he dealt with a fucking child's tantrum and wouldn't give in to the irritation that crawled up his neck.

"And the woman? Who was she?" he asked.

Alex's ears rang and his spine cracked him ramrod straight.

"You got all stiff when she approached. Stiff, not a stiffy." Hunter didn't even flinch when Joss drove an elbow into his side.

"She works there. She's not important," Alex answered over the pounding in his head.

The mates met each other's looks like a perfect fucking triangle around the table. Alex could see the gears grinding away in their brains.

Nope.

"We're done here," he growled. He chugged his hot coffee, ignoring the burn, and threw the mug into the sink. He turned toward the door to hide his wince when the mug bounced and shattered.

"Alex," Tansey scolded.

He raised a middle finger and kicked the door open. She could call him out on being an asshole. Better that than putting words to the air he didn't want to consider.

Mate.

Fuck him. He'd seen it enough with the others and people in town. That dopey, doe-eyed look that left slobber on their chins from the slack-jawed awe they felt when their other half was found.

The strong, strange pull he'd felt for Liv after

being turned made sense when he knew what the hell a mate was to a shifter. How long had he spent huffing her clothes or sniffing at all her bottles in the shower? That unknown, wild thing eating away at his insides had grown obsessed.

That frightened him more than anything. More than waking up after he should have died. More than walking out of the woods naked and half insane with more questions than answers.

Liv's scent and the longing he felt in his bones for her scared him shitless.

Claws ripped through his heart. Fur pressed against his brain. Each step he took toward the barn was agony.

Fuck the bear. He'd had one hell of a time tripping his own feet to keep from turning right toward Liv from the moment he knew she was in Bearden.

Alex shook his head to clear her face from his mind. She'd let his secret out and now everyone was up in his business. He didn't want to sit through another interrogation with all those worried eyes probing into him. And he sure as hell didn't need Liv up in his shit.

Except the look of hurt on her face ripped him apart all over again.

He'd lashed out. He'd let her think awful things. Again. They'd been down that road before.

Whatever. He would take on all her anger and hate if he kept her safe and away from him.

Yeah, he was an asshole. He deserved whatever he got, not the love and devotion the rest of the clan flounced in. He'd spat in the face of his future.

Because he was a monster.

His bear rolled through him strong enough to force him to his knees.

Too wild. Too angry. Out of control animal like him wouldn't be changed or tempered or domesticated. He'd hurt anyone that got too close. Maybe not in the first hour, but days? Weeks? He was a ticking time bomb. There was no putting the pin back in him.

Monsters did monstrous things. Even if he wanted her, even if he gave in to the danger he brought to her life, he'd done too much damage. He'd hurt her again and again.

There was no salvaging the garbage fire of his life.

CHAPTER 7

"...And that's how it happened. I didn't mean to reveal any sensitive information." She'd fucked up, in polite-speak. Royally. Epically. Whatever other words described her monumental mistake.

Liv had requested the meeting as soon as she'd walked herself into her home, then spent the rest of the night and weekend imagining all the various ways she'd get fired and the resulting fallout. Yelling and security called on her. Stern disapproval and marched out the doors. Picturing the smug look on her mother's face when she was forced to return home, jobless, was the worst of them all.

Rylee jotted something on her notepad. "And your connection to Mr. Carter—"

"College boyfriend. We ended on bad terms, so it was a shock to see him in the program. I didn't want there to be any unpleasantness between us." Liv forced herself to keep her chin lifted and eyes looking straight ahead. She was responsible for her own mess. She'd accept whatever came from making it. "Instead, I caused unpleasantness and revealed his participation in the program."

She didn't care if she had to beg. She wanted to keep her job. Selfish reasons aside, the research facility was a unique opportunity.

Rylee frowned and shifted in her seat. "Well, technically you didn't. If what you said are the words you used—"

Liv blinked back against the thread of hope. "They are."

"Then it was the clan that put two and two together." She snagged Liv's eyes and held her in a steady, no-nonsense gaze of pure maternal disappointment. "Take this as a hard lesson, Liv. You're in a different world now. Ears might be listening to your every word, no matter how quiet or roundabout you might say them. Not just locals, either."

The last was muttered and Liv raised an eyebrow. Rylee pressed her lips together, gave a small shake of her head, then took off her glasses and pressed her fingers to her eyes.

"It's not just your run-of-the-mill protestors out front. Our program is being spied upon." She placed her glasses back on and tapped a stack of papers on her desk. "Our local Supernatural Enforcement Agency office heard chatter from some hunter cells about reversing the shifter 'contagion'. They've asked me to verify the authenticity of seized documents."

Hunters. A chill ran down Liv's spine. Even without growing up as a shifter, she recognized the danger. Hunters wanted to eradicate all supernatural life and were comfortable with everything between outright killing to adding in a whole lot of suffering beforehand.

Liv sank back against her chair. "We have a leak?"

"This is a small town; some information about what we do here is bound to get out."

Point noted, Liv tried not to squirm in her seat.

"But yes, it seems someone is pilfering actual research and handing it over to hunters." Rylee sighed sadly. "I wish I could say I was surprised. Those that want to do harm to our supernatural friends always have a way of digging their grubby fingers into things. This was the first enclave to reveal itself and seems to be an epicenter of activity because of it."

With a clearing of her throat, Rylee swung back into brisk determination. "No matter. We've survived worse than some pages falling into the wrong hands. We'll make it through this. That's our superpower. We're still standing and living our lives, no matter what gets thrown our way."

The attitude was admirable and Liv took solace in Rylee's optimism. "Happy to help in any way possible," she said.

"And how are you settling in, outside of outing one of our volunteers?" Rylee tempered the soft teasing with a smile and adjusted her glasses. "I like to check in with our new hires. This seems as good an excuse as any."

"Oh, uhm." Liv wracked her brain. The question blindsided her. The revelation of a leak within the facility seemed more important than if she felt at home. "Good, I suppose. Just trying to find my place with everyone else on the team. They've been here longer, and it's never easy being the new kid in the lab. They ambushed me this morning with a plan for a trail ride this weekend."

"Trail ride? Huh. I'm sure you'll have a wonderful time." Rylee slashed her eyes to her notepad. "Well,

I've taken up enough of your time. Back to work with you."

The others were already hard at work by the time Liv buzzed herself into the lab. She lifted fingers in greeting to the few faces that glanced up from their tasks.

Liv settled in at her desk. She went through the ritual of plugging in her earbuds and cranking up her music, then opened a series of files to review the last trials. She felt a little sick to imagine someone else with dangerous motives sifting through the same documents. Even worse, she may have met the person who handed them over.

The entire premise of the serum was to reverse changes on a genetic level caused by the bite of a shifter. A contagion to anti-shifter groups. A fascinating process to everyone on the serum team. Those changes left visible markers in a subject's blood—ridges around the cells that weren't present in pure humans or shifters born with an animal inside them.

The actual process was more involved than switching something on or off again. That where she and the others on the team stepped in. Genome editing allowed genetic material to be added, removed, or altered within particular locations of a subject's makeup. The bite of a shifter was a catalyst. The research team wanted to figure out another catalyst to nullify the first. When the bite held the potential of death, a reversal serum could save lives.

Liv tapped her finger against her lips as she scrolled through the research already conducted. She tagged a few places and printed out page after page of sequences. With those, she marked and circled and added notes of what she wanted to try or compare to previous work.

She lived for being in a lab. Most of the time, it was just theory. But those theories sparked more ideas and discussions on what was possible. The science field was an ever-shifting, uneven staircase of progress. What seemed like magic a hundred years ago was used as a common building block in current research.

She'd loved it from the moment she opened up her first chemistry set, to miniature volcanic eruptions, and all the way through the years of math and science courses and defending her dissertation. She couldn't imagine not working to find more questions to answers about the world around her.

Liv jumped at a tap on her shoulder and hastily removed an earbud.

"Hey," Jenny said. "We're all breaking for lunch. Care to join us?"

"Yeah. Be there in a sec," Liv answered.

Was it her imagination, or did Jenny eye her screen a little too long before turning away?

Her imagination. Balls. Jenny had access to the same findings. She'd have no reason to spy over a shoulder.

Liv closed out of her computer and joined the team in the break room. Most were already seated and digging into their lunches. Leela excused herself to find something in the cafeteria. Liv tracked her from her spot at the microwave.

"What was your meeting about this morning?" Jenny asked, popping a grape between her lips.

All eyes turned to her. Too curious? Too unconcerned?

Liv shook off the unease tightening her shoulders. "Oh, nothing important," she said lightly. "Dr. Strathorn just wanted to check in and see how I was adjusting."

Not a lie, but not the whole truth, either.

"And you told her everything was good, right? Otherwise," Chuck sliced a finger across his throat, "we'll have to take care of you."

The others snorted or chuckled.

Liv raised her hands in mock defeat. "They won't get a word out of me," she promised.

The others lapsed into discussing their weekend activities and future plans. Jokes and teasing were tossed back and forth while Liv eyed the others from under her lashes. She didn't want to believe anyone in that room was capable of betraying their project. Working with a group that wanted to destroy others went against everything she believed in.

But Rylee's words still stuck with her even as she laughed around a bite of food. Someone had leaked information.

Any one of them could be a spy.

CHAPTER 8

Alex flicked the long line and pushed Lula into a faster gait. Her ears turned and twitched at his every noise, as well as the bleating of the calf in the paddock with them.

The mare had been slower than usual on the last trail ride, then listless the next day. He'd pulled her from the lineup and kept a close eye on her, but all signs pointed to her recovering from whatever ran through her system. Probably just feeling mopey over being forced to work. Damn horses were moodier than the vampires living under Bearden.

Something warm and hard crashed into his knee and he stumbled before catching himself.

"Dammit, Daisy," Alex muttered. He shot a glare

at the calf slowly stepping back to wind up another attack.

The little calf butted him again, then took off after the horse. Lula whinnied and turned from a trot to a prancing walk. Daisy slowed her run to copy the move, complete with an impressively loud moo. Then she took off again with a leap that took all four cloven hooves off the ground.

"Okay, okay, you little punk. I know what you want." Daisy stopped at the sound of his voice and flicked her ears in his direction. She was born in the first wave of calves for the season, but had been rejected within a couple of hours. He'd raised her by hand ever since. Every season saw at least one or two calves who needed extra tending. Alex always volunteered for the job.

Alex pulled a few alfalfa pellets from his pocket and both Daisy and Lula turned for him. Lula stuck her nose right against his chest and pushed. "Greedy monster," he chastised. He ran a hand down her neck as he gave Daisy her treat, then switched and scratched Daisy's ears while Lula nibbled out of his hand.

Animals were easy to understand. Humans were where everything went wrong.

Automatically, Alex pressed back on the urges

and faint sendings from his bear. He didn't want to think about Liv.

Across the yard, Ethan stepped out of the main house and adjusted his Stetson on his head. Then he trudged off the front porch and didn't stop until he leaned against the paddock fence.

Well, shit.

He'd avoided everyone since the disastrous breakfast days ago. They'd surprisingly given him space, too, and hadn't hounded after him to give in to their demands for peace and love and all the bull-shit that went with it.

"How's she doing? One of the others threw a shoe this morning and there's a kid who has his heart set on her. Apparently, Tansey is now posting pictures and fake profiles on the ranch website. Lula here likes long stalks of hay on the beach."

Alex almost smiled. Almost.

First he'd heard of another horse needing a new horseshoe, though. "She's fine to go."

Ethan took off his Stetson and rubbed a hand over his head. Balls. Alex recognized the motion as one made right before there was a big ask.

"Jesse is running late. Think you can help load up the mounts and haul them to the mountain trailhead?"

Alex frowned. He kept as far from the trail rides and overnight guests as possible. Courtesy for Ethan. He couldn't keep his head on straight, which was a dangerous combo with cameras and jumpy humans. Mixing with them was trouble he didn't want to bring down on the ranch.

He could be considerate sometimes.

Besides, most of the guests were just salivating over seeing some shifter lose his shit. Alex didn't appreciate being another sight on a damn safari.

He eyed Ethan and scented the air, feeling like something was brewing. His involvement with the research facility was still a sore spot. Days of quiet didn't mean the matter was settled.

"I suppose I can help haul them," he said carefully.

"Good. I'll pull the big trailer around and we can clear out the barn. There's a big group today."

Alex led Lula back through her stall and shut Daisy out in the paddock. She had her own stall to slip into if she got tired of running around like a giant puppy. Lula, he gave an extra handful of oats for cutting her vacation short.

By the time he had her brushed down and ready to go, Ethan pulled to a stop outside the double doors. Together, they led most of Black Claw's horses as well as the mounts borrowed from the neighboring lion pride into the trailer. Those loaned horses made the entire trail riding business possible. Ethan was slowly building his own herd of horses, but extras were still needed. That was where the lions came in. Trent Crowley hated humans, but had the horses. Ethan ran the trail rides, Trent provided the mounts, and they made a partnership filled with tension and demands.

They were on the road for barely a full five minutes when Ethan shot Alex a look that had him regretting ever stepping foot on the ranch.

"So that trouble the other day—"

"Isn't up for discussion." Alex rolled his head to the side. "I know you force everyone else onto these little drives to get their feelings out. Too bad for you because I don't have any."

"No, not you. You're just a raging pain in everyone's ass. You make everyone else around you suffer."

Alex spread his hands wide and pasted on his most infuriating smile. "If the shoe fits."

"What happens if you get your wish and drive everyone away? You act like you don't need anyone."

"I don't." His inner bear growled in an echo of his irritation.

Ethan gave him a flat stare. "You didn't know the first thing about what you were when I found you. Even now, I don't think you have a clue what you're doing. You need a clan, probably more than any of the others."

"Yeah, I need to fuck up more lives."

"It's not always about what you can offer someone else. Sometimes you need to lean on someone else. You need someone to ground you and pull you out of that dark hole."

Ethan's look bored into him, but Alex braced himself against the encouragement to talk. Fuck talking. He had a beast under his skin. He knew the danger he brought to the table. He wouldn't put that on anyone. Ethan was insane for bringing him to Black Claw in the first place.

The rest of the ride stayed blessedly silent. They were the first to arrive at the trailhead, as planned. He knew the others didn't like the guests all up in their business while they unloaded mounts and prepped gear. Too many cooks in the kitchen.

He and Ethan worked quickly to bring the horses out of the trailer and secure them in neat little rows. They were just about done when the first car slowly eased up the road. Ethan left Alex to finish settling the horses while he went to greet the man and woman.

Another car arrived and more guests joined Ethan's little group.

Then a third pulled up, music blasting even through the closed windows. The back door creaked open and Alex jerked upright as he inhaled a tangy scent.

Sweet and tropical, coconut and flowers, exotic and familiar.

Liv stepped out of a car packed full of people and jerked to a stop. A hand behind her shoved her forward and broke their stare. She scowled and whirled away.

Alex lifted a lip and snarled at the man exiting the car.

An elbow jammed into his side. "Behave," Ethan growled under his breath.

"What the fuck is this?" he demanded. He twisted around to face his alpha, bear boiling under his skin and pressing against every inch of his mind. "What did you do?"

"Got a call from Rylee about a group coming from the facility and a guest one of my clan should avoid." Ethan's phone rang, and he held up a finger to silence Alex's objections.

Yeah, fuck that. "What, Ethan?"

"Yep," Ethan said to the person on the other line. He stalked away and glanced over his shoulder at Alex, then studied the trees again. "I'll head back once you get here."

Alex glared, suspicion prickling up and down his spine.

Ethan shoved his phone back into his pocket. "Listen," he started, "something came up at the ranch. I have to back out of the ride today."

Alex growled. "Fuck you, Ethan. I work better with animals than humans. There's a reason I don't do these."

"We're all just animals, buddy. It's high time to push you out of the nest. Fly free, little bird."

"At least animals are honest in their doings. They don't need any dirty tricks."

"Didn't I just see your little calf head butt you when your back was turned?"

Liv laughed at something one of the others said. The noise of it punched him in the gut. He couldn't stick around with her there. He couldn't be near her.

"I don't have a horse." Alex bit down on his tongue for inserting the tiniest quaver of desperation.

Ethan pointed to his own regular mount.

"Patches has four legs. I made sure to slip your saddle in with the rest."

Down the road, the front end of a truck appeared. Alex bit the insides of his cheeks. Fuck. He needed to do something to get out of the trail ride.

"You're trusting me with your old nag?"

"Like you said, you're better with animals than humans. Doubt you'd hurt him on purpose." Ethan turned and walked backward, still calling out advice. "Clear your pockets if you have any food in them. He's a thief."

Jesse pulled to a stop and slid out of the driver's seat. Ethan beat a quick path to his second, took the keys from Jesse, and hauled himself behind the wheel almost before Sloan dropped to the ground.

Motherfucker.

They were all in it together.

And they called *him* the asshole?

"Hey, Alex," Sloan greeted with a wave of her hand.

Yep, send the SEA agent out on the trail. He could see the protection against his potential misbehavior not-so-subtlety strapped to her waist. If he was lucky, she'd miss her shot and give him a dose of silver straight to the heart.

Alex stared after the puff of dust from Ethan's tires.

"You going to get to work?" Jesse asked from right behind him.

Alex jumped. "You know I'm going to be shit at this."

Jesse shrugged. "Probably. But these suckers are all stuck in town with you, so they might as well learn who to avoid."

"And the kid that wanted Lula?"

"Oh, he and his folks are booked in a couple weeks. You think Ethan or Tansey would let you near a child?"

Alex made a noise of annoyance. His bear echoed the sentiment. "I'd never hurt a kid. Joss and Hunter are going to let me around their cub."

"Joss is high on pregnancy hormones and Hunter is just as crazy as you are. Not really the best measuring stick." Jesse dipped his hat to a passing guest, then moved past Alex with a deliberate knock of his shoulder. "Come on. Got people and horses to see to. Faster we get started, faster we get home."

CHAPTER 9

A lex bit back a sigh and the urge to pass a hand down his face. There was a reason he didn't deal with guests. They were idiots. Their idiot actions poked and prodded at his bear.

"Foot in the stirrup. Other one." He swallowed his irritated growl. "Now stand up and swing your leg over."

Over the back of the horse, he watched Jesse look around for the next rider to assist. His gut twisted when the only one still on the ground was Liv. Jesse took another look around, then stepped toward her.

Alex's bear snarled at the other man. Unmated, just as unattached as himself. A threat.

No one belonged anywhere near Liv but him.

Alex shook the thoughts away. Not his own. Not

logical. Liv had her own life. He didn't need to get involved.

He handed the reins to Chuck and blindly strode toward Liv. There was nothing else in the world. No other guests. No horses in his way. Just Liv, and the man walking toward her.

Jesse spotted him and found somewhere else to be.

Alex came to a stop right behind her and coughed. "You good?"

Liv jumped at the sound of his voice. She pressed her lips together like she had a thousand things running through her head and didn't know which one to say out loud. Finally, she gestured to Lula. "She keeps moving when I try to get up."

"Lazy nag," he chided. Liv pulled back sharply, and he rushed to explain. "Lula. She's succeeded in getting a little time off by faking being sick. I guess she still doesn't want to get back to work."

Liv's lips twitched. "Been there."

"Like that time you came back from visiting your folks at Christmas and couldn't drag yourself back to the labs? Thought you were going to fail out that semester."

"Yeah, just like that." Liv laughed softly, a thin

thread of embarrassment entering her tangy, tempting scent.

Danger, danger. He touched too close to good times and pleasant memories. His skin itched and muscles tensed.

Alex dipped his chin to his chest and took a step back. "I'll hold her steady while you mount up."

Liv killed her laugh. Her eyes turned guarded when she nodded. "Thanks," she said stiffly.

He grabbed hold of Lula's halter. Another dip of his chin gave Liv the okay to try mounting once more. As soon as she stuck her foot in the stirrup, though, Lula danced her ass end in the opposite direction. Liv wobbled, halfway off the ground.

Alex shot a hand forward and landed on her lower back. "Steady."

Heat spread through his palm. Fire licked through his arm. An inferno burned up his spine and settled in his brain.

Mate.

Bite. Mark.

His bear rolled through him and slapped him in the face with a sending powerful enough that he clenched his fists against the onslaught. Liv, dark hair tickling his chest and her laugh filling his ears. Fuck, he missed her smile. He missed *her*.

The bear wanted her. The sending evolved from his own memories of her to the hopeful future. Short hair bobbed around her chin and did nothing to hide the savage scar on her shoulder.

Alex twisted at the images. Savage scar, short hair, yes. Fear in her eyes and dread in her scent.

He wasn't good for her. He'd hurt her.

His bear slashed at his middle and roared in his head.

Alex threw off the beast's desires and locked him away in the back of his mind. He cleared his throat and stepped back, breaking the connection with Liv as she swung up and settled into the saddle. "Here are the reins. She's a plodder, so don't expect to go galloping all around. She likes neck rubs and being told she's beautiful."

Dumb fuck. Shouldn't have opened his mouth.

He whirled around and stalked over to where Patches waited with a back leg cocked in mocking ease.

The first ten minutes of the trip went as well as possible, he thought. They made it out of the parking lot.

Even the second ten was a success by his standards. He hung back at the end of the line and hunched his shoulders against the peals of laughter and teasing from the group. But he didn't throw himself from his horse or let his bear take his skin.

A half hour more ticked by while he willed the time to pass quickly and without incident. He shoved his bear to the very, very back of his mind and pled disinterest in the surrounding conversations that sounded much too loud.

At least the view was nice. He lifted his gaze above the bouncing heads of all the other riders. The green canopy of the mountain woods broke often enough to let through sun and bright blue sky. The peaceful sight helped calm him and keep his mind off the intoxicating scent that seemed to overpower everything else.

Passing along one edge of the lake, Jesse pulled to a stop and waited for the others to plod ahead and Alex to catch up. "You're quiet," he said after a moment of riding next to one another.

Alex slashed his eyes to the other man and glared. "Was this the plan all along? Strand me out here and make me talk to her?"

Jesse leaned an arm on the saddle horn, cool ease disregarding the venom in Alex's voice. "I don't pretend to know the thinking of our alpha."

"But you'll support the idiocy anyway."

"Of course. He's my alpha," Jesse snorted. "But

that doesn't mean I blindly follow. I'm his second, Alex. I'll question him when I think he's wrong and back him up when he's right. I'm sure he has his reasons for throwing the pretty little female in your path."

Alex waved a hand. "Have at her. She's not mine."

"Take that up with your bear and your own eyeballs. You haven't stopped staring at her since you noticed she was here. You want her, even if you won't admit it to yourself." With another snort, Jesse heeled his horse forward and joined the next clump of riders. He said something Alex didn't bother to listen to, and they cracked up with laughter.

All but one.

Liv glanced over her shoulder.

He wanted her. Yeah. Fuck yeah. From the moment he'd laid eyes on her. And for whatever reason, the brilliant woman put up with his shit. He was an army brat who liked playing in the dirt and didn't see much use in making nice with dipshits. Wild, she used to call him with a small smile lighting up her eyes.

Then his world was torn apart, and he put up walls and trenches and miles of barbed wire between them to keep her safe.

Only, now she was in Bearden. She knew what he

was. She worked with his kind. The danger of her knowing and rejecting was gone.

His bear rolled through him and pushed at all his resistance. Alex shoved right back.

He was the only danger to her, now.

The biggest one of all.

Fuck it. Her sweet scent clogged up his nose and all his good sense. He wanted to taste her, to feel her, to pull her into his bed and never let her go again.

He pulled even with her.

Then another scent invaded his nose. The sour stench curdled his stomach and brought his bear roaring to the surface with the urge to rip and fight.

His monster.

The odor was stronger than what was left on those damn deathday cards. Newer. If he had to take a guess, the fucker had passed through within the last day.

He felt like he was drowning. Nowhere to turn. Nowhere to escape. He was as trapped as he'd been six years ago, feeling jaws crushing down on his arms and legs. Days of pain. Weeks of thinking himself insane. The yearly, taunting reminder of how his life changed for the worse.

Liv looked up at him, grey eyes welling with

concern. And that moment, he understood down to his very cells what he brought to her life.

Breathing hard, he heeled his horse to the front of the line.

Couldn't get near her. Not now. Not ever.

Not when he had a monster watching for him.

He wouldn't put her in his path.

LIV STARED at Alex's retreating back and slowly shook her head. "The fuck did I do?" she muttered.

Hot and cold. More hot than anything, but not even in an approachable way. And the cold was as bitter to swallow.

She hated the pang in her heart whenever she got close. What was the misquoted definition of insanity? Repeating actions, but expecting different results?

Yeah. With Alex, there would always be trouble. Expecting anything different was on her.

The only other guest that wasn't part of her group sawed at her reins and nudged her horse forward. She'd arrived with the other rancher, Jesse, but she didn't look comfortable riding and hadn't inserted herself into any of the conversations up and down the line.

"Don't blame yourself," she offered. "He's been in a bad mood for weeks."

"Years, I'd say." Liv tried to crack a smile and failed. Screw him for making her hope and hurt. She was better off keeping him at a distance. "Call me Liv."

"Sloan. I'd shake, but I'm afraid I'd fall off."

Up ahead, Jesse wheeled around. Critical eyes latched on to Sloan and he waited for them to catch up. "You'll have more luck if you sink down and relax your core. Let your back sway with each step."

Sloan followed the instructions but didn't look any more comfortable. She narrowed her eyes. "You've done this before."

"Almost like it's my job. Ladies." He touched fingers to the brim of his hat and kicked his horse after Alex.

"Don't ride very often?" Liv asked.

"I've been on a couple tours around Black Claw. This is my first one longer than an hour. I can already tell my mate's going to be drawing me a bath and giving me a massage tonight." The grin she gave said the pain was worth it.

Mate. There was that pang in her heart again. The term was new to her, but ranked high on the list. A good few of the volunteers had mates of their own. The ones she'd come in contact with were obviously in love. There was something undeniable in the way they seemed to orient themselves toward the other person, even across rooms and through walls. Then when they were together, their faces just lit up.

She was glad Sloan and the rest of the lucky ones had their somebody. She just wished their happiness didn't make her loneliness peak.

Liv took a cleansing breath and tucked her hair behind her ears. "I didn't know Alex would be here, or I'd have avoided it entirely."

"I've never been much one for avoiding something on account of someone else. They can handle it, or they can't." Sloan cocked her head to the side. "So what's the deal with you two, anyway? If you don't mind me shamelessly sticking my nose in your business."

"Nose away," Liv chuckled. She liked Sloan's backbone. "We dated for a few years in college." Up ahead, Alex stiffened. Good. He couldn't stand to be around her or say a nice word, but he could certainly hear. "Thought everything was good. Then I went to a conference and came back to no ride at the airport."

"Oh, no."

"It gets worse. When I finally got home, he'd cleaned out all his stuff. I got a text a few hours later saying he was leaving. No shit, Sherlock. I think the missing clothes and other items explained that much."

"That's... Wow. I didn't think it was that bad. Mouthed off about the wrong thing and you had enough, or something, but not going dark."

"Mmm." Bad was watching him move on so quickly and keeping focused on her final weeks before graduation. Bad was still not fully understanding what happened to make him leave.

Liv glared in his direction. She'd tried to be the adult. She'd given him a warning that she was in town and a chance to explain his actions. He'd crumpled both up and thrown them back in her face.

Fine. No big deal. She didn't need to see him after the stupid trail ride. Talking to him was a thing of the past.

The words and affirmations felt as hollow and flimsy as her heart.

"But hey, at least he didn't hold you up at gunpoint. Or get you mixed up in his psycho ex's revenge plot. And you haven't had to deal with any murderous family members or coworkers." Sloan winked. "We're a fun lot, let me tell you."

A shocked noise bubbled out of Liv, followed by a longer laugh. "I have... so many questions."

"Ask away. It's only fair."

Sloan stuck by her side for the rest of the ride. By the time they arrived back where they started, Liv's stomach and cheeks hurt from laughing so much. Sloan avoided talking about Alex, but the rest of the clan were easy targets for ridiculous tales.

Alex kept to the opposite end of the line through it all. She gritted her teeth when he silently took her horse's reins. His nostrils flared and a look of disgust passed over his face before he turned away.

Fine, if he wanted to play it that way. Liv kept her mouth shut at the wave of disappointment that rushed through her.

Sloan crunched up behind her, thumbs stuck through her belt loops. "Me and the girls—Tansey and Joss, that is—have an irregular gathering. We kick out the guys, bust out the nail polish and terrible movies, and drink ourselves rotten. Or rather, that's what Tansey and I do at the moment. Joss is about to pop, so she just sighs and mothers us in preparation for actual motherhood."

"Are you sure?" Liv shot a glance in Alex's direction. She narrowed her eyes when she caught him spinning away. Newfound determination coursed through her. Screw him. She lived in Bearden, too. He wouldn't keep her from making friends and living her best life. "You know, that sounds pretty awesome. When are you next getting together?"

"Right on. Stick it to 'im." Sloan grinned. "I need to double check with the Mistress of the Guestbook, but I think next weekend."

"Well, have your people call my people," Liv joked. She gave a final wave to Sloan and joined up with Jenny and Chuck for her ride home.

Liv pulled up short when Alex stepped in her path.

"You should leave," he growled.

"You don't have any say in that," she snapped back. She tried to step around him, but he stepped back in front of her.

"You're not safe here, Liv."

"Because there's some hulking huge asshole blocking my path."

"Not me. There's—" His growl cut off his words, and he passed a hand over his face. "I don't want you here, okay?"

Liv made a noise in the back of her throat and

tried to brush past him. Again, he followed her movement like they were dance partners. What a joke. They'd fallen out of step long ago.

She dodged his attempt to block her. "Good thing we don't need to see each other again, isn't it?" she called over her shoulder. She locked his response on the other side of the car door.

Asshole. Jerkface. Dingus. The common curses didn't seem enough for the annoyance of Alex. She had to get creative for the twatface fartsicle. He wanted her gone? He could fuck off with that demand.

The car door opened and yanked her out of her thoughts of voodoo dolls and petty revenge. Liv forced on a pleasant smile while the others loaded inside. Pulling out of the parking spot was the best feeling in the world.

"So, how was it? All the nature and horse smell you can stomach for a lifetime?" Jenny asked, glancing in the rearview mirror.

Liv glanced back as the car started to pull away, then turned to answer Jenny's question. "Entirely unexpected."

She must have imagined the look of longing on Alex's face.

CHAPTER 10

Alex slid through the night, black fur blending in with the darkness all around him. This was his home. His comfort zone. The others had their happy lives and lived in the daylight. He was a beast made for the dark.

He prowled forward, knowing exactly where his path led him. The light at the end of the tunnel. The pot of gold at the end of the rainbow. Both things impossible for him to touch, but he still continued forward.

Stupid. Idiotic. He would have been better served if he locked himself away for the next eternity instead of giving in to his raging bear and letting the beast take his skin. Maybe he wanted to lose that last shred of willpower to convince himself he wasn't the one in the driver's seat. He wasn't responsible for where the bear took them.

But he knew what the bear wanted. He wanted her, too.

Then there was the looming, terrible fact that jumped out at him. He wasn't alone in Bearden.

The monster of his past lurked somewhere in the night, too.

Going to Liv's, even watching her from a distance, wasn't safe. Alex played with fire, but he couldn't stop himself from lighting the matches.

And he still couldn't resist her.

He circled the cluster of tiny cabins the research facility rented for their scientists and staff. He didn't have any difficulty picking out which one belonged to Liv as soon as he got near. Her tropical, delicious scent grabbed him by the scruff and demanded he step closer.

He was almost at the back porch when the door swung open and she stepped into the night air. Her scent billowed around her and wafted toward him.

He nearly chuffed with pride before backing away from the light. Not his.

But his legs wouldn't move. His bear wouldn't let him leave.

So he watched the gorgeous woman stride across the concrete slab to the small grill in one corner. She set her plate of food and balanced supplies on the flimsy side tray, lifted the lid, and started the flames. Once she put the steak and potato on the rack and closed the lid, she slipped back inside and returned with a beer that she sipped while staring up at the stars.

He remembered the first steak she'd tried to cook. It'd been his birthday, and she'd wanted to surprise him. He'd showed up to their date amid the sound of smoke alarms and a building-wide evacuation. The surprise nearly burned down her apartment. He'd brought her back to his place and taught her how not to set fire to the city block while she protested making him do all the work on his special day.

That night was the first time she stayed the night. Special, indeed.

The back door of the cabin next to hers opened, and another figure stepped into the night with a bag of trash. She stomped to the bin and deposited the bag before waving. "Evening, Liv!" the other woman called to her. "Up to anything tonight?"

Liv dropped her eyes, startled. The quick beat of her heart calmed down a second later. "Hey, Jenny.

Just making dinner and maybe catching up on some shitty television."

"If you're up for it, we might play some cards later. I'm sure Matt would love to see you there." Amusement coated Jenny's voice.

A hint of embarrassment entered Liv's scent. She rolled her eyes and waved the other woman back inside. "See you guys at work."

Alex wanted to tear the world apart.

She had a life. Friends. Colleagues.

Dates.

The twinge of pain in his chest didn't mean shit when he'd left her. Of course, she'd moved on. He'd wanted that for her. She couldn't spend her years tied to a crazy bear who needed to be put down.

A growl leaked out of his throat in a vicious rumble. At himself. At whoever dared get close to her.

She belonged to *him*.

Liv turned and looked right at him. Alex froze, caught in her gaze.

But no. She squinted into the night. "Someone there?" she asked softly.

He wanted to step out of the darkness and go to her. Let her touch his fur, see it melt away until it was just him standing in front of her again.

Except he'd never again be just himself. The growling, snarling other half would always be along for the ride and always want to take a bite out of her.

Bite. Claim.

Mate.

No. He put a halt to the thoughts and pulled back the paw inching forward.

Too wild. Too out of control. He couldn't be trusted with her.

She was brightness, and he was relegated to the shadows.

Alex pried control away from his bear and turned away from the light. He circled her cabin, staying to the shadows. He couldn't be the one by her side, but he could make sure the bastard that made him didn't get near her. She didn't deserve any further pain and suffering. He'd ambushed her with a lifetime's worth already.

Cabin checked, he forced himself to leave his temptation behind.

He ran through the night, but there was no putting distance between himself and the past.

He neared the ranch when he felt them. Other bears and their bullshit. He didn't want to deal with them. He growled a warning, but neither peeled away.

Hunter and Lorne flanked him. One clipped a back leg, and he swung his head around to unleash a furious roar. The second he turned, the other rammed into his side. Alex tumbled to the ground in a heap of snarls and limbs.

He gathered himself quickly and squared off against the others. Two on one. They needed the numbers. He fought like a cornered animal on a good day. That moment, he wanted to murder the entire world.

He roared again, letting loose all the frustration and fury that'd built up since he last unleashed on them. He wanted Liv. He wanted her safe. He wanted to be rid of his monster. He wanted a normal, happy life.

Nothing went his way.

They charged him at the same time. He braced himself against the blows and lashed out with wicked claws. The ground rumbled under their feet from the force of the slapping, slamming battle.

Blood scented the air and whipped his bear into even more of a fury. Bite. Roar. Claw.

Kill.

Death rode on his shoulder. He should have long succumbed. Instead, it ate at his heart and made him want to spread it everywhere.

Hunter slowed and stumbled. Alex tore into the weakened beast, biting and slashing. More blood spilled and slicked the ground under their paws.

"Are you done now?"

Alex whirled around. He snarled when he spotted Ethan. His alpha regarded him coolly and silently, but didn't move a muscle. He knew the danger he jabbed and taunted.

"Shift, Alex. That's a request. Next one will be an order."

He snarled. His bear snarled. Ethan could lick his furry balls.

His alpha's eyes glowed like shards of silver. "Shift," he said.

Power infused the word. It started as an itch in the deepest part of his ears, then spread through his brain and fired all the synapses in blinding unison. His bear was burned away to nothing, and the charred remains puffed away on a breath of air.

His shift ripped through him at the order. Fur melted back to flesh, bones snapped and reshaped. His muscles, already tired and sore from the constant need to shift and fight, shook under his skin.

Alex gritted his teeth and pushed himself to his

knees. Fuck dying in the dirt. If Ethan was going to put him down, he'd be upright.

"Why the fuck did you put me on the trail with her?" he snarled.

"Because she's important," Ethan answered simply.

"You've been more of an asshole since she showed up," Lorne muttered.

Hunter threw him a lopsided grin. "Congrats, man."

Alex flicked them all off. "She's not what you think."

Mate.

His bear joined in with the insistence. Sendings shoved at him until he couldn't ignore them any longer. Liv, happy and smiling, just like he remembered. The only difference was the savage scar marring her creamy skin.

Ethan still looked on stoically. "You've been fighting it for years, haven't you?"

Alex didn't say a word. It was all he could do to keep himself still against the clenching pain in his middle.

"Stop fighting for once. Give in."

He cocked his head and bared his teeth. "Because you're such an expert on accepting what's given to you." He rolled his eyes to the others. "All of you. You dug in your heels and fought every step of the way."

Alex shoved to his feet. His heart ripped to shreds. Important. Yeah. Liv had always been important.

Important enough to keep safe, no matter his personal cost. Didn't they understand? He was a master at setting his world on fire to keep her warm.

"You're different now. You know what you are." Lorne said quietly. "If she's your mate, you won't hurt her."

"Truth speaker," Hunter agreed.

Alex shook his head. "Already have. There's too much there to forget."

"So don't forget," Ethan rumbled. "Grow."

Alex turned his face to the stars, just as Liv had done. Stop fighting. Grow. Bullshit advice he couldn't act on. He wasn't the only obstacle to overcome. Even in a perfect world where he didn't have some rogue bastard stalking him, he'd done enough damage.

But... she'd approached him. Instead of surprising him with her existence, she let him know she was in town. Instead of giving up when he was a dick to her all over again, she tried to buy his goodwill with drinks and more convincing.

He wanted to believe his story wasn't at an end. He wanted to ink more chapters with Liv in the starring role.

He also wanted a normal fucking life without someone sending him deathday cards every damn year.

Alex took a stumbling step into the darkness while his bear roared. "No."

CHAPTER 11

Liv sifted a hand through her hair and leaned on her elbow. She looked between the findings on the computer screen and the notations she'd jotted down. Something teased her in the results. She just didn't know what she was looking for.

She was glad for the work. The puzzle of genetics and the added challenge of altering a sequence without harming anything else was a fine distraction from the other trouble on her mind. One man in particular whipped through her head at any sign of weakness. She did *not* want to think about Alex. She'd allowed him to live in her head rent free for far too long.

Liv rolled her eyes at herself and redoubled her focus on her work.

A shoe scuffed somewhere behind her. She glanced at the clock. Too soon for anyone else to find their way back from lunch.

Liv spun in her chair and peered through the glass partition on the lab door. "Someone there?"

Silence answered her.

She'd seen enough horror movies to know going right back to work asked to get axed from behind. Liv pushed to her feet and slowly stepped toward the door marking the separation from desks and lab space. She couldn't see anyone when she leaned against the wall. Even craning her neck, she didn't spot anyone.

No other sound, either.

She reached for the keycard in her jacket pocket. The reader beeped in recognition and she pushed inside the deserted lab.

No one stirred. The work stations were blank with screens of sleep.

She felt movement behind her just as a large shadow covered her. Liv whirled, heart pounding as paranoia turned to fright in a squeal.

Alex chuckled and set smoldering eyes on her. "Easy, it's just me."

Liv bristled, heart still thudding in her chest. She didn't know if she was more annoyed at the sight of him or that he'd spooked her. "What are you doing here?" she gritted out.

Alex raised his hands. "I just—"

"How did you even get in here? This is supposed to be a secure facility."

One half of his mouth hitched up in an infuriating smirk. "Through a door, just like everyone else."

She could have clawed out his eyes. Instead, she reached for the nearest phone and started punching in the number for security.

"Liv, Liv," he laughed. He fished into his back pocket and flashed a card between them. "Relax. I have a pass."

"You should have returned it downstairs. You're done here, remember?"

He blinked slowly. "I may have been a little hasty."

"Well, I'm hastily deciding to end this conversation. Drop off your pass on your way out. I have more important things to do than fight with you." Liv swiped her card again and yanked open the door.

Alex slammed a firm hand against the door and slipped between her and her exit. "I'll let you take my sample. I'll even withdraw my complaint against you."

"You made a formal complaint?" Asshole! Her hair rustled with the force of her shake. "You know what, that doesn't matter. You're done. I can't take your sample. It wouldn't be right since we know each other and you hate me."

"I don't hate you," he said immediately and almost too quiet for her to hear.

Almost.

Her heart pounded again, but fright wasn't the cause.

Liv took a step back. She folded her arms over her chest and stared at him for a long moment. "You're welcome to stay in the program. I'll even arrange for someone else to collect a sample. They're all at lunch right now, so it might be a bit."

"No can do. Now or never. I'm on a tight schedule today. Errands to run and doctors to piss off." He copied her crossed arms, but the lean against the door made him look cool and relaxed instead of annoyed. "Besides, it's no different than donating blood for the doctor down at the clinic. Small town. Everyone knows everyone."

Liv looked over her shoulder and willed someone

else to walk through the doors. They remained irritatingly closed.

"Fine," she agreed. "But only if you agree to get back on schedule for these visits. And someone else handles you."

His eyes danced with mischief. "Oh, Liv. You of all people should know no one can handle me."

Infuriating man. Jackass. Utter goblin.

Liv favored him with a tiny nod of acceptance before stalking across the lab to wash her hands, snap on a pair of gloves, and open a kit for sample collection. Done, she pointed to a chair. "Sit."

"Two stars. Your bedside manner could do with a little improvement."

Liv glared at him until he pushed off the door and sauntered toward her. Sauntered.

Pustule. She hoped he had a year of infected toenails and blistered heels.

"About to be five stars, commendations for heroic efforts but alas, deceased patient if you don't sit down."

"Mouthy."

At least he took a seat. After passing much too close and flashing her a cocky grin.

Liv grabbed herself by the back of the neck and forced her focus back on her work. He was nothing to her. No one. Just another patient she wanted to drain into a dry husk and be rid of forever.

She ripped open one of the wipes in the collection kit. He held out his arm, green eyes hidden by lowered lids. Even though she couldn't see them, she felt him watching her. That awareness shivered down her spine.

She swabbed at his skin. So close, she could smell him even over the chemicals. Pure male, like the outdoors and some intoxicating combination of soap and shaving cream. She almost leaned closer and inhaled him like a creep.

No, Liv. He's *the shifter.*

His eyes followed the path of her fingers before he abruptly turned away. "I've been told to extend you an invitation to the movie night. Sloan made me promise to stop in while I'm on the supply run."

"Ah, so that's why you're here. Not of your own free will."

He moved suddenly and nabbed her wrist before she could turn away. Green eyes snagged her own, brightening as his fingers stroked over her skin. "I was a dick to you," he said gruffly. "You didn't deserve all that."

Holy hell, the touch felt good. Heat whipped through her. She doused it with cold reality. He'd hurt her. He had someone else in his life. She'd already tripped down the path of having that other relationship thrown in her face.

She tugged away from him and dropped her gaze. "Did you apologize to Daisy for kissing me?"

His infuriating smirk returned again. "She doesn't need any apologies."

"Open relationship? How progressive of you."

"I don't share," he growled. His eyes flared brightly once more. He reached into his pocket again and pulled out his phone, tapped the screen, then turned it around for her. "This is Daisy."

Liv stared at him blankly until he dipped his eyes to the screen. With a heavy sigh, she glanced down. "You're kidding me."

A tiny calf shoved her nose toward the camera. The rest of the photo was filled with a black face and one half of an ear.

"You raise cows?"

"Rancher, remember? Cows and horses are my bread and butter." He swiped the photo and showed another of the same calf rolling around with all her legs in the air. "You saw her before. When you made your surprise visit."

Liv's cheeks warmed. The visit hadn't been the only surprise. They'd been just as close when he turned the confrontation into a kiss that burned her to a crisp.

"Didn't you also threaten to turn her into a steak?"

"She knows what she did." A sappy smile appeared on his face as he swiped through more photos. Daisy's set switched to a different calf, nearly fully grown and all black except for the tongue licking at its nose. "I take care of the ones that have trouble. Problems with their health, or if they get rejected. It's hard to let those ones go, so Ethan lets me sell them off for someone else to start their herd or to use for like, 4-H projects or something."

He looked like a proud father showing off his kids.

Her ears rang, and she busied herself with checking over the rest of the collection kit. She knew what was inside. She'd verified the contents after the first snap of her gloves. She just didn't want to face the hurt that sank her stomach.

So many potentials and possibilities had been imagined while they stretched out in bed together. Kids were one of them.

Liv broke open the swab pack. Cheeks first. Then hair. Blood came last.

After that, she could feel weird without him around. A good ten minutes hiding from the world in a bathroom stall felt about right.

"Open wide," she murmured.

Alex smirked again, but did as he was told without remark.

Liv was glad by the time she peeled off her gloves. Being surrounded in a cloud of Alex's smell brought back too many memories. Making it through all the little touches necessary to perform her job without running in the other direction felt like the hardest thing she'd ever done.

Freedom was in sight. One pesky ex-slash-volunteer to get rid of.

"Do you not like it here?"

"What?" She blinked at the sudden question.

"The others went to lunch, you said. You didn't. Do you hate them?"

When she turned back toward him, he was close. Far too close. If she closed her eyes, she imagined she could feel the heat blasting off his chest. Just a few inches and she could close the distance.

She backed away toward the door between the lab and office.

"No. I just had some work I wanted to do. Which

is still waiting on me." She nodded to the hallway door. "You know the way out."

Alex followed her. "Let me feed you."

"You want to take me to lunch?" She rounded on him, utterly dumbfounded. Frustration and shock mingled together into a messy, rotten sludge. The sheer audacity of asking her out after breaking her heart. "What makes you think that's a good idea?"

"Nothing, that's why it sounds good." Cocky smirk back on his face, he took another handful of steps after her.

Liv huffed a laugh. Wild Alex. Always a surprise with him.

"Thanks for the offer, but I really need to get back to work." She swiped her key in the reader and yanked open the door. A hand shot over her head and held it open.

She twisted around to face him again. "Wrong door."

"I can't leave until I know you're going to the stupid movie night. The mates will skin me otherwise."

Liv shrugged. "Might not be a bad look."

She ignored him stepping after her. She took a seat and tucked herself into her desk, still ignoring his presence behind her. He had to give up eventually, right?

Mail had been delivered while she'd attended to him in the lab. Liv reached for the thin stack in her inbox when Alex's hand shot out and snatched the top letter out of her fingers.

She spun around in the chair to catch him stuffing the envelope under his nose. A growl ripped out of him, hard and ferocious, and stilled her movement. Shifter. He wasn't just the wild man she remembered. He was more than that, now.

Alex inhaled loud enough for her to hear. "Who sent this?" he demanded.

"I don't know, you have it in your hands."

"Have you gotten others?"

"Again, in your hands." She reached for it then and he growled when she tried to take it away. "Alex, take it down a notch."

His eyes flashed dangerously, but he killed the rumble in his chest and pulled the envelope away from his nose. His lip lifted in a silent snarl and he ripped it to pieces in his haste to get at the letter.

She couldn't spot a return address between his fingers and sighed.

"What?" he asked in a too-loud voice. "What do you know?"

"It's mail, Alex. We all get them. They get scanned and checked for threats before being passed along to the recipients. If it's not business, it's probably something from a protestor inviting us to a church service to hear about how we're damning our souls working here."

"This is nothing like that." His eyes brightened until they glowed. "You're coming back to the ranch with me. Get your things."

"That's not happening."

"Liv, *now*."

She pressed a hand to his chest. Holy hot damn, he was on fire. Not literally, but touching him felt like his temperature was through the roof. The heat spread through her, just like it'd done when he caught her from stumbling on the trail ride and earlier, when she took his samples.

She shook her head to clear the haze. "One, I'm working, Alex. Two, there's no way I'm going anywhere with you."

"You're in danger."

The macho Neanderthal attitude sparked a war inside her.

The primal, needed-to-get-laid side of her lolled out her tongue at the display. Strong, fierce man wanted to keep her safe.

The logical, who-the-fuck-was-he-kidding side cut through the bullshit. He'd apologized for acting like a dick. He'd showed off pictures of the cow he let her think was his girlfriend. But those tiny acts were nothing compared to the crater of hurt he'd blasted the day he left.

She couldn't trust him. That was the painful reality. He'd given up every ounce of trust and goodwill when he couldn't be honest about why he left.

And she was an idiot to get anywhere near him again. She didn't want to get burned. She couldn't go through another round with him.

"Yeah, you said so before." Liv rolled her eyes. "Or was that just because you were trying to drive me away? I'm curious, do you still want to get lunch or are you just looking for someone you can order around?"

She plucked the letter from his hands and quickly scanned its contents before crumbling it at tossing it in the trash. "This is nothing but more of the same. Getting warned away from the enclave is pretty common for everyone in the building."

She was saved from more growly objections by the team returning from their lunch break. Their laughter and good mood died as they passed through the door. Too many eyes passed from her to Alex and back again on a continuous loop.

"Everything okay?" Matt asked.

"Alex was just leaving. We have a kit to process this afternoon," Liv said smoothly.

"Liv—" he tried once more, a hint of concern in his green eyes.

Screw his concern. He didn't have any for her years ago. She didn't need it now.

"Thanks for stopping by. Please call next time to make sure someone else is here to help you." Liv sank back into her seat and spun away from him. The others quickly made way for him as he growled out the door in a huff.

CHAPTER 12

He was being stalked.

Deathday cards were one thing. The asshole knew where to send them.

Showing up in his enclave, his town, was something else. An escalation. One Alex couldn't abide. The fragile control he maintained shredded into nothing while the bastard remained at large.

Find him. Kill him.

He wanted the nightmare to end.

And Liv... Liv was a complication. A distraction. One he couldn't afford. Someone he couldn't put in the line of danger.

But she already was.

He replayed all their interactions since she

showed up on the ranch and uncorked all the bull-shit he'd bottled up. Each one ended in rejection. But the frequency and the high emotions, plus that damn kiss... Somewhere, he'd put a target on her back.

And he couldn't keep away. He tried telling himself he just needed to check for his monster's scent, but a deep voice in his head called him a fucking liar.

Liv wasn't safe. Not from him, and not from his monster.

The thoughts didn't curb his instinct to protect. She was his. Had been for years. He'd just been wise enough to stay away. Now that she was so near, there was only one direction for him to move.

Closer.

But she wasn't at the cabin. She was all the way back at the ranch, safely stashed away with the other mates.

Her place was safe. Quiet. No sign of his monster.

Yet.

Alex put his nose to the ground and ran. Through trees. Along the river. Out of the mountains and back toward the ranch.

Track him. Find him. Kill him.

The triple desires morphed from the litany he'd recited since he'd been changed. Another objective added to the list.

Keep Liv safe.

The ground churned under his paws. He ran and stopped. Sniffed. Ran again.

The perimeter of the ranch was coated in familiar smells and small tufts of fur. Black Claw, all of them. His clan. His people.

Frustration built inside him as the night wore on. Nothing out of the ordinary reached his nose.

His muscles burned by the time he doubled back and ran toward the living quarters. Two big structures sat on a hill overlooking the land. A short distance away were the huts for the rest of them. Unease crept up his spine as he slowed his pace.

He wanted more than the empty home he'd walk into, the cold bed that waited for him, and the dull throb of his temples.

But he had more to do before going back to his dark home. Bright lights spilled out of the main house in a cheery sort of way. If he listened hard enough, he could hear the faint murmurs of feminine voices. The mates were gathered inside. While they talked and drank and did whatever secret girl shit that required signs on the doors declaring NO BOYS ALLOWED, he ran the perimeter and made sure they were safe.

Alex pulled up short.

There. Faint. No less rage inducing as the tiny thread he'd inhaled on the trail.

His monster.

He backed up and tried to catch a trace of it again, but the stench vanished like a wisp.

Old. Too old to track properly, but that didn't stop him from trying.

Frustration and fury roared a challenge into the night. Monsters hid in the darkness and under beds. He wanted to shine a bright light on the bastard and finish him off. No more waiting for mysterious cards to arrive. No more dreading sleepless nights or the nightmares when he finally gave in. He wanted to close the entire, painful chapter and write a new book with red ink.

He'd gone after Liv. The line was crossed. His fate written in stone. His bear shoved sendings through his mind of blood and death.

Alex pushed his nose to the ground again. Five feet, maybe less, was all he could track. Another snarl sawed in and out of him with every breath.

How? How had he gotten onto the ranch without anyone knowing? Where the fuck was the rest of his trail?

He paced the spot. He pawed at the dirt. Marked the area with his own presence because he'd be damned if he let the bastard take even a square foot of land from him.

There was a soft chuff to his left and he rounded on the noise. Alex raised his lips in a vicious snarl before he recognized the small party of four big bears.

His clan. His people.

Ethan stepped out in front of the others and dropped his head to the ground. Hunter, blond fur a stark contrast against the dark night, shoved his way past Jesse. Jesse gave a warning growl, then took a sniff before stepping away for Lorne to pick up the scent.

Ethan growled and the bears split. Jesse and Lorne ran in one direction. Ethan and Hunter took another. His own bear still snarling away with visions of red death, Alex took off after his alpha.

Didn't matter how big of an asshole he was to them, they still had his back.

Fuckers didn't deserve his trouble, same as Liv.

They had lives. Most of them had mates. He brought danger to their doorstep.

Only one way to repay that debt.

Track him. Find him. Kill him.

Protect the clan.

Keep Liv safe.

CHAPTER 13

Liv carefully sipped her beer while Tansey applied the last coat of black polish to one hand. The other was already done and one nail smudged, but the pile of chips next to her was well worth the trouble.

In the background, a Brat Pack movie played out a teenage drama and coming of age story. Joss claimed she knew every line of the script and Liv secretly fist-bumped her in solidarity.

Across from her, Sloan pressed a button on the blender. The room was big and opened to a spacious kitchen. Necessary, from what she understood. The rooms upstairs regularly filled with guests for the bed-and-breakfast side of the business Tansey and

Joss ran. They needed all the stove burners they could get.

Bear heads were carved into the railing posts and stood guard over the stairs. Exposed beams and wood walls kept with the cabin theme and made the open space feel cozy. The giant fireplace helped, too. Though it was empty, Tansey promised she was welcome to sit by it when the weather turned cold again.

Liv didn't doubt for a moment that the offer was real and not just an empty idea. The women of Black Claw were refreshingly honest and open.

"I'm going to die if you don't hurry up," Joss wailed dramatically. "I'm going to die if those cookies aren't done soon, too."

"None of us are attending your funeral," Tansey teased. Joss stuck her tongue out in answer.

Sloan poured the blended drink into a red plastic cup. She stuffed a straw into the slush and garnished it with a tiny umbrella before presenting it with a flourish. "For our mother-to-be," she announced.

"And done." Tansey's lips twitched with the grin she tried to hide. "Guess you're an honorary Black Claw now."

"Good. Maybe Alex will stop being such an a-hole." Joss gazed longingly at the contents of her drink before slurping on the straw. She groaned with pleasure and rolled thankful eyes toward Sloan. "I can't even tell the difference."

"That's because your taste buds are faulty," Tansey snickered.

"We lose our heightened senses when we're knocked up," Joss lamented to Liv. "Can't shift, can't smell, can't taste."

"Ain't motherhood grand?" Sloan teased as she added alcohol to the blender and remixed the drink to her preference. "I guess that means the normies outnumber the freaks."

"This freak will still bite your face off before you can even think about pulling your gun," Tansey said in a sing-song voice. She punctuated it with a raised middle finger, which Sloan answered with one of her own.

"I guess I'll just drink this all on my own," Sloan countered.

"Can I trick you into bringing me another bottle, then?"

"Ooh, me too, please and thanks," Liv added.

Sloan nodded along, then brought nothing but her own drink back with her when she settled on a couch next to Joss.

Tansey sighed heavily and pushed to her feet. She

crossed into the kitchen, tucked two bottles under her arm, and grabbed another bag of chips to add to the spread. Liv reached for the offered beer, but Tansey jerked it just out of reach.

"Now that you've taken guest right and been initiated properly into our cabal of troublemakers," she said, "you have to dish. Alex. What the hell? What did you do to turn him into a raging assbutt?"

Liv squirmed under the attention that swung her way. "He's always been like that. Never could keep his mouth shut when needed."

"Well, dammit, Liv. There go my dreams of peace and quiet," Tansey scolded.

Joss giggled. "As if either of those things exist when you're around."

Sloan gave her a high five.

Liv took the bottle when Tansey held it out a second time and mulled what she wanted to say. The past was in the past and, despite her bumps and bruises, there was no changing it.

The present was simply confusing.

Avoiding her and telling her to leave turned into a kiss turned into walking away like she didn't matter. A meltdown at the bar resulted in more running away and hurt. Cold shoulders were just as painful.

And then there was the visit to the lab. Night and day, hot and cold. She didn't know what to make of it.

Of anyone in the enclave, the women she sat and drank with felt the safest to speak her mind. She didn't need to worry about coloring their opinion of Alex; they already had a vibrant understanding.

"He got weird the other day when he came by to relay Sloan's invitation."

Sloan's eyebrows arched in confusion. "Relay what now?"

"The invite," Liv repeated. "He said you made him promise to ask me over."

Sloan shook her head, eyebrows shooting together. "I never asked him that. I was going to shoot you a message, but he told me he ran into you."

"Outright lies. Bet you wish you weren't so human now, huh?" Tansey said into her bottle.

"You're missing the bigger point." Joss hugged a pillow to her stomach and wiggled in place. Her voice fell to what Liv could only describe as a yelled whisper. "He made sure Liv came over!"

Tansey pointed to the redhead. "Put a pin in that." She switched focus to Liv. "Explain 'got weird.'"

"He freaked out over a letter I got at work. Inhaled it hard enough I thought he'd suck it right up his nose, then demanded that I come back here with him."

"Did he?" Tansey asked softly.

"What do you know?"

"I shouldn't say—"

"Well, that's some double standard garbage right there."

Tansey made a face. "I don't know everything. Hell, I don't think even Ethan does. Alex gets worse this time of the year because it's when he was turned. And the rogue who did it taunts him by sending shit in the mail."

Silence hung heavy in the room until Sloan muttered, "Shit."

"But you were bitten and you're not..." Liv trailed off.

Liv's heart tightened with pity. He'd hurt her so much, but she wasn't made of ice. Clearly, he struggled. Tansey gave her even more insight into that horrible time. Alex didn't seek out a shifter. The change had been forced on him. There was no quick healing, either, when the bastard kept reopening the wound.

"Crazy? Struggling? Pushing everyone out of my way every single damn second of the day?" When Liv nodded, she shrugged. "I still struggle. But I also had my mate from the very beginning. Alex was on his own. That he survived was a damn miracle."

Mate. Hearing the word with such reverence was becoming commonplace, as was the longing it triggered. The word and talk of Alex made her head spin even more than the drinks she'd had over the course of the night.

Sloan dipped her chin, seriousness etched across her features. "Part of our job at the SEA is to make sure those deemed a danger to society are treated humanely. Packs and clans have a chance to step in and handle the problem first, but we're there to act if they don't. There's a reason why it's a death sentence to forcibly change someone. They don't always make it out whole. Sometimes they're too far gone."

Joss reached forward and squeezed her hand. "He's stubborn. But I think you are, too. Maybe he'll open up about what happened with you."

"I think that ship has long sailed." But she made a silent wish that no one in that room or wherever the men had been banished had to deal with such a final outcome as death.

She was saved from any more probing by the oven dinging. Tansey and Sloan were the first to their feet and into the kitchen. Tansey proudly pulled out a tray of cookies and waved a hand over the obscene shapes.

Liv giggled at the penis cutouts, but it was the one in the very center with extra bits of dough arranged in a splatter at the tip that was the masterpiece.

"Now I can truly tell you all to eat a dick."

Tansey beamed a proud grin at her. "That's the Black Claw spirit!"

LIV TUCKED an arm under her head and watched the final scenes of the movie without really taking it in. Her head still felt a little fuzzy and her stomach was deliciously full. Few dick cookies remained by the time the other woman started nodding off.

The front door creaked open. Liv glanced up to see Alex raise a finger to his lips and jerk his head for her to follow.

Wanting to see what he was up to, she eased to her feet. None of the others stirred.

She ghosted after him into the kitchen. Almost as soon as she did, three others streamed through the door. Polite nods all around, but the men had eyes on their targets. Hunter scooped Joss up, and she snuggled against his chest as he walked right back out the door. Tansey and Sloan were roused enough to make it to their own feet and wave tired farewells before being ushered off to their beds.

Which left her alone with Alex.

"Were you out there all night waiting on us?" she blurted.

Something uncertain flickered in his eyes before he hid it away again. "We patrolled," he said gruffly. "Had to make sure no one snuck up on you ladies in your delicate states."

"Delicate." Liv snorted. "Just tipsy."

"Better work on that, then." He opened the fridge and pulled out two beers. Once he popped the tops and handed her one, he slid to the floor and stretched his legs out with an air of casual sexiness.

Liv cautiously sank to the floor opposite of him. Silence made the air hard to breathe. Or maybe it was just being around him when he wasn't ping-ponging between high emotions. Liv picked at the label on her bottle, unsure of what to say as the years of distance spanned the space between cabinets.

"Been a while since we've done this." Alex tipped his head back and took a long pull from his bottle, eyes still locked on her.

Late nights after the party wound down, they'd

find themselves nursing their last drinks on a kitchen floor. So many deep conversations happened then. So many plans for the next day. Where to get the best breakfast for a hangover, for starters. Maybe catching a movie after. Where they saw themselves in ten years.

"Mmm." She took a sip of her own beer. "Even before... everything."

"We got busy. Spending Saturday nights at a house party just wasn't it anymore."

"Part of growing up, I guess. Saturdays at home weren't so bad."

"No," he said, one corner of his mouth lifting in a cocky smile. "Not bad at all."

Cheeks warming under his scrutiny, Liv ducked her eyes. So much had changed, but some stayed exactly the same.

Wanting off the memory train, she took another sip from her bottle and quirked an eyebrow at him. "Is there really a calf?"

"You saw her."

"I saw a picture of one on your phone. Give me five seconds, and I can get one of those, too." She bit her lower lip. "Besides, I have reason to not believe you."

She expected a flare of anger in his eyes or a

complete shutdown. Maybe a mocking grin and some snippy comment. She didn't expect him to spread his hands wide and tilt his head to concede the point.

"You have every right to question me." He stood suddenly and held out his hand to help her to her feet. "Come on. I'll prove it to you."

Maybe it was the alcohol or maybe her innate curiosity. A firm tug on her heartstrings over their past and what she'd learned about him. The jumble of reasons killed the alarms blaring in her head and she slipped her hand into his.

Warmth spread through her fingers and palm. Nerves sparked to life as she stood mere inches from the man who'd been her greatest love and biggest hurt. Liv's breath caught in her throat as she stared up into his eyes.

"Let's go," he said in a deep rumble.

Alex ushered her into the darkness and closed off the light of the kitchen. A low hum of bugs chirped in the night, quieted only for a split second by the call of an owl. Night in the mountains was nothing like the city.

Something primal scratched at her brain. She was alone in the night with a predator.

She turned her head slightly. "I can't see anything."

Firm hands landed on her shoulders. "Don't worry." His breath ruffling her hair. "I have you."

And he did. Alex guided her forward slowly. His hands never strayed away from her shoulders. Even after her eyes adjusted to the darkness, he was right there, pushing her gently toward the barn. A dull thrum of loss sank her stomach when he dropped his hands and cracked open another door.

This time, he led her through the dark. His fingers wrapped around her wrist and he dragged her in his wake until light suddenly bloomed overhead.

They passed by horses sleeping where they stood, heads hanging low. One or two tossed their heads, but quieted when they went unacknowledged except for a quiet, "Hush."

Alex didn't stop until he reached a stall at the end of the row. He leaned against the half-door and nodded inside. "Meet Daisy."

The same calf he'd threatened when she first drove up to the ranch was curled up inside. At the sound of his voice, she jerked her head up and blinked big, sleepy eyes at him. The moment quickly passed, and she sprang to her feet, bonking her head against the stall in an effort to get closer to Alex.

"Okay, okay," he chuckled. He eased open the latch on the door and stepped into the stall. Daisy shoved her head into his hands and he scratched her ears. He lifted his eyes to Liv, a smile stretching his mouth wide. "You want to pet her?"

"She seems awfully attached." He did, too. He was more relaxed than she'd seen him and his smile hadn't dropped in the slightest.

"She's an equal opportunity attention whore. Come on in."

Liv let herself into the stall and shut the door behind her. Daisy twisted and turned around Alex, leaning into the spots he scratched. When he let up, the little calf turned her attention on Liv and knocked her legs hard enough to make her stumble.

"They're like really big puppies," Alex explained, eyes twinkling. "No painful bites, but you still have to watch for the tongue."

As if to prove his point, Daisy's tongue flicked out and wiped up his arm.

Liv laughed. She dropped to her knees and scratched the calf's sides. Daisy huffed and leaned into her. When she glanced up, Alex was slipping out of the stall.

"Where are you going?" He shrugged and disappeared out of sight. Liv turned back to Daisy. "Guess it's just you and me now, cow."

Daisy pressed her nose into the crook of her neck and mooed. Liv couldn't hide her grin if the world depended on it. The calf was absolutely adorable.

Alex returned a second later. "Here. She loves these."

He dropped a few green pellets into her palm. Liv didn't get a chance to see what they were before Daisy mooed again and stuffed her face into her hand. Liv laughed again at the rough tongue tickling her skin.

"Come on," Alex said again. "I have some sanitizer in the tack room."

"So you do have another woman in your life," Liv teased as she pushed to her feet.

"Demanding wench used to keep me up all night, too." He glanced down at her while she passed through the stall door. He slid the latch back in place. "Jealous?"

"Supremely. I love the smell of farm animal in the morning."

He felt… warm. Open, almost. Definitely playful.

Watching him with the calf thawed icy places in her heart.

That, in turn, made her sad and regretful. And yes, a little jealous. What did life on the ranch, with all those other people and even the dang cows, too, have that she didn't?

Liv stayed quiet as she followed him into the room at the end of the aisle.

Saddles and other equipment were neatly stored. Even a few shiny trophies were displayed on a shelf high on one wall.

Alex pumped his hand under a dispenser attached next to the door. Liv followed the actions, noting the way the muscles of his arms tensed and flexed with each delicate movement. Oh, she could dig in her memory for long-ago anatomy lessons for the names of muscles and joints. But those weren't the reasons why her heart suddenly pumped a healthy dose of fire in her veins.

She tore her eyes away and swallowed hard when he stepped aside. She foamed herself up with sanitizer and washed away grime picked up from petting Daisy. Too bad the questions and warring desire stuck with her.

Liv flicked a glance to Alex. He watched her,

expressions shuttered. "Thank you for showing me your calf."

"Least I could do. I didn't want you thinking I'm some cheating asshole."

No, he was just the kind of guy to leave without a word.

Oh, hell. The night had gone relatively well. And she couldn't get Joss's words out of her head. Maybe he'd open up to her. She desperately wanted that to be true because deep down and uncovered by a wash of drinks all night, she wanted to believe there was still something between them.

"Alex," she started, voice barely above a whisper, "what happened?"

"Not tonight, Liv," he sighed, sounding tired. His shoulders slumped, and he didn't look at her. "Not now. Not while—"

He cut himself off and turned his back on her. A growl rattled in his throat. Liv stepped to his side and touched her fingertips to his jaw. Just that small pressure vibrated his growl through her and down her spine, where it settled hotly in her core.

So much pain. She'd seen the anger, but he'd kept the pain stashed away in their interactions. Her heart hurt for him. For who they used to be. "I want to know."

His voice dropped to a pitch of pure gravel. "It's my life."

"It was *ours*."

"I know." He shoved his hands in his hair. "I'm working up to it, okay? It's not a happy story. It still isn't. There are things happening right now. Bad things, horrible things, and all I can think about is—"

Another growl. Another cutoff. He jerked his chin out of her reach and squeezed his eyes closed, but she stepped in front of him. "What?"

Alex's nostrils flared and his eyes blazed green when he opened them. Heat burned in the sharp color. They were the eyes of a predator who'd found his prey. "You."

Just like before, something snapped in him. Some thin thread of control couldn't contain him and he struck, fast as a snake. Liv exhaled the moment he wrapped an arm around her waist and dragged her flush with his body.

He was hard everywhere. Chest, abs. Her pulse thundered in her ears loud enough to block out the end of the world if it happened right at that moment. Maybe it did, and she just didn't care.

"I thought I could be near you without touching. Or tasting." Alex pressed his lips to the crook of her neck, grazing her with his teeth and sending a shiver down her spine. "You just smell too fucking good."

"Wha—" she began, voice shaking. Liv licked her lips and tried again. "What do I smell like?"

"Tropical, like coconuts and flowers." He skimmed his nose up her neck and nipped her earlobe. "Under all that? You smell hot and wet."

Liv caught a sound in the back of her throat before it spilled past her lips as a helpless mewl. She shouldn't have worried. Alex was there to devour the noise for her.

His hands cupped her cheeks, thumbs stroking over her cheekbones as his lips crashed over hers. He started slow and immediately cast it aside on a strangled note and a firm lick into her mouth. She met him stroke for stroke, tongue tangling with him like she needed him to live.

His hands dropped, but he didn't stop touching her. He directed an inferno over her skin. Fingertips gliding up her arms sparked desire to life. Squeezes to her hips, her ass, boiled her blood. When he dipped under the hem of her shirt, fire heated her skin.

She arched into his touch when he finally cupped her breasts. A pleased growl sawed out of him when he peeled down the cups of her bra and rolled her hard nipples between his fingers. Each tweak and touch arrowed need straight to her core.

When his mouth wasn't on hers, he licked and sucked a path down her neck and over her shoulder.

"Alex," she groaned. His hand skimmed up her inner thigh. 'No' and 'stop' were the farthest words from her mind. 'Please' and 'keep going' were more accurate.

He pulled back suddenly, but she pressed her palms to his cheeks and forced him to look at her. His eyes blazed that bright, inhuman green. The shade wasn't far off from his natural color, but the glow to them sent her pulse racing.

He spun her around and slammed her hands on the wall. His booted foot kicked her legs apart and then he was there, right where she needed him, palm grinding against her. Even through her jeans, maybe because of them, she quaked.

"This what you want?" he snarled in her ear. She felt every inch of him when he rocked his hips into her.

"Yes," she moaned. She tossed her head back and rolled her hips against his trapped cock. *More*, she silently begged. *Need more.*

Alex ripped down her zipper and laid another

biting, sucking kiss on her skin. "Christ, Liv. I can fucking taste how bad you want this."

Holy hell. He'd been wild before, but this was another level. His growl vibrated right through her and dialed up her need up to eleven and broke off the damn knob.

And when his fingers slid into her, she was lost.

Pressure built steadily as he thrust in and out of her. His growls, too, heaved out of his chest as much as her breath heaved in hers. Fuck, but she loved that sound. The dirty, animalistic nature of it wound through her and shoved her ever closer to a release she knew would shatter her apart. Knew, and craved.

He nipped at her skin again, harder than before. Sharper. She sucked in a gasp at the sting of pain.

Alex snarled, long and low. The noise of an animal, not a lover.

Liv froze the same moment he reared back.

"No." Strangled, smothered, garbled. All described the word that blasted out of Alex.

He stumbled back a step. A louder snarl left him, sounding just as terrifying as the last. Liv twisted around to see his eyes brighten to an impossible color before he stalked out of the room.

"Alex." He didn't stop. She followed him and tried to get his attention again. "Alex."

Daisy mooed. The horses woke and tossed their heads, eyes rolling in fear. Some crowded away from the aisle, others neighed loudly and kicked the doors of their stalls.

Alex turned back one last time. His eyes still glowed, but there was nothing of the man left in them.

He strode into the night and let loose a savage roar.

Liv swayed with the cold rush of abandonment.

Hot and cold. Troubled beyond everything she figured. She couldn't let her guard down around him.

Something wet chilled her skin. She dabbed at her neck and gasped when her fingers came away with a tiny smear of blood.

What in the damn hell?

More confused than ever, Liv straightened her clothes and started back toward the big house.

CHAPTER 14

Alex drummed his fingers against the hood of his truck as another car eased past. Still no sign of Liv and his bear was growing anxious. His skin felt tight and he itched to brush his fingers over her soft skin. Or give in to the press of fur against his brain and let the bear take control.

He gritted his teeth against the beast's unease. He'd let him have too much control. Leaving Liv aching and needy was a fucking disaster. One he couldn't repeat. One that deserved a full grovel with apologies made in words and actions.

If she ever showed up at her home again.

Another set of tires crunched on the gravel drive and he drummed his fingers against his truck again. Balls. He leaned back against the windshield and let his Stetson fall over his eyes, the picture of casually waiting. *Nope, no inner animal tearing him apart here.*

Fucker.

His bear prowled through his head and pressed against the walls Alex had carefully and sternly put into place.

Two more cars passed before one slowed and turned into the spot next to him. Liv's tangy scent reached him even before she opened the door and his mouth twitched in an involuntary smile. Finally.

His bear backed down a tiny bit. Not enough for any actual peace, but enough to think clearly.

Alex stayed seated on the hood as she stepped out of her car. He wanted to jump down and go to her, press his nose against her skin, inhale that sweet scent until he died, but the angry glint in her eyes said he'd receive a much-deserved smack.

The idea held him back, but only just.

"What are you doing here?" she demanded.

Alex cracked a smile and shrugged. "Be glad I'm on two legs and didn't show up on four and break through your back door."

Liv's jaw tightened. A tiny grumble worked its way out of her throat and she stomped away from him.

Fuck. "Liv, wait." He hopped off the hood of his

truck and stuffed his Stetson back on his head. Three strides later and he cut her off. "I fucked up."

"You could say that again," she muttered darkly and tried to slip past him.

"I fucked up," he repeated and spun around to follow her, "and now I'm here to apologize. I also brought a peace offering."

Liv paused with her keys dangling from her door. She pressed her forehead to the wood for a count of five before turning back to him, arms crossed over her chest. One raised eyebrow commanded him to speak and to make it fast because she wasn't entirely sure she wanted to deal with his bullshit.

It was a fair assessment. He didn't want to deal with it most days, either.

"Since you weren't at lunch the other day when I stopped by the lab, I assume you're still a workaholic and you haven't eaten yet today." He held up a bag from Tommy's Diner. "It's not Hank's Fun-n-Buns, but it's infinitely better."

"I'm a vegetarian."

Alex's face fell. Well, fuck. There went that plan.

Liv snorted back a giggle. Then she gave up and laughed, complete with a pointed finger. "You should see the look on your face. A vegetarian. Like I'd kicked your dog. Or calf."

"You're just busting my balls." This woman... He should have known. He'd spotted her grilling a damn steak.

"You're the shifter. Aren't you supposed to be able to smell lies or something?" She turned back to her door and twisted the keys in the lock.

"Not when you have me so distracted." Alex leaned against the wall next to her and quirked an eyebrow. "Are you going to invite me in?"

"Is that another deep, dark mystery of yours? You're a secret vampire, too?"

"You know they don't need invitations, right?"

Liv rolled her eyes and opened the door wide enough to slip inside. "Meet me around back. I'll bring some plates."

She didn't trust him in her territory. He understood why and still hated it.

Licking his wounds, Alex rounded the house. The porch was exactly the same as before. Bite-sized living, though he didn't judge. His own hut on the ranch wasn't much bigger. The small grill still stood in one corner. A plastic table and two chairs pressed against the side of the cabin. He took a seat in one just as the back door opened.

Liv took a seat across from him, two plates in her

hands. Her fingers twitched, but she didn't make any move to pass him one. "So, this apology."

An apology, and more. She needed to hear every last detail.

That was the real peace offering. The food and apology for getting her worked up for nothing got him through the door. Or rather, on the porch. But there would be no moving forward until she knew what happened in the past and why he was still a fucking mess that'd hurt her all over again.

His bear shoved forward with a rough growl. Alex couldn't tell what bothered him the most—thinking about the circumstances of his arrival or hurting Liv.

Alex leaned back in the flimsy chair. "I don't know if I can get through this without needing to shift. It's not you," he quickly added.

"Sure seemed like me the other night."

"That *was* you. But only because you're hot as fuck." She sucked down a sharp breath and he pushed on. "I didn't lie, Liv. I can't get you out of my head. Haven't since you showed back up. Getting close to you isn't enough. I want more. I need it. And not in a whiny, desperate sort of way. I wake up craving you and fight through the rest of the day hard as a fucking diamond."

Her pupils blew wide and her pulse kicked up a notch. Calmly, like he couldn't smell the hint of arousal mixing in her scent, Liv set the extra plate in front of him with a clink. "So explain why you left me in the middle—"

"Of the best orgasm of your life?" he smirked.

"If you're not going to take this seriously..." Liv pushed to her feet, gathering her plates up again.

"Liv." Alex shifted uncomfortably in his seat. Looking over the back yard didn't do shit to calm him. Whoever said nature was a positive influence on one's mood was a fucking moron. He wanted to tear apart the bag of food, the stupid plastic chair, the table and porch and entire house, while he was at it.

He inhaled and exhaled. Liv's scent rolled over him like a balm. He had no right to that, not after everything he'd done. "I went camping while you were away, just like we planned. Nothing seemed wrong, until it was. A bear came out of nowhere and attacked."

Liv sat back in her chair. "But it wasn't just any bear."

"No." Alex swallowed hard. "Not just any bear."

The minutes, hours, and days piled up in painful memories. He could still feel fire burning through his limbs. The wounds on his arms and legs and chest closed up and sealed his blood back inside him. The sick, stuttering beat of his heart steadied out, grew stronger.

A low growl rattled in his throat. Liv reached forward and squeezed his hand.

She had no reason to trust him or believe him. Support? He'd chucked that as far away as possible and followed it up with a flaming arrow. The good that had existed between them was long gone and he was an idiot to expect otherwise.

And yet... her hand rested on his and offered him a lifeline while his story threatened to pull him under.

"I still don't know why he targeted me. I didn't know what was happening. This was all before shifters and everything else weird and spooky came out of the coffin, so to speak. One minute I thought I was dying, and then everything hurt. I couldn't control my body. I felt like one of those firecrackers you light on fire and the ashes burn like some wiggling worm. That first shift was fucking agony. And then I was a bear."

Huge paws. Claws made for death. His first stumbling steps had been accompanied by the desire to rip and tear into anything that moved. Then he'd caught that bastard's scent. Some deep part of him knew and tried to process the reality. Bitten and changed. Made anew. All at some fucker's whim.

Alex clenched his fists and forced words out of his mouth. "I thought I'd gone crazy. You have to understand that. Nothing prepared me for that moment. I was even less prepared for the fury that came with it. The beast in me has an overwhelming drive to fight and bleed, and it started the moment we caught the scent of the rogue that changed me. Days gone at that point, but my new drives didn't give a fuck. All the bear wanted was to find him and kill him. We ran and ran until my paws bled and it hurt to breathe. That was when I took back control and forced a shift back into human form. Naked, starving, feeling raw all over my body and mind. It took another day to find my way back to my truck."

"And that's why you left," she said finally.

Pity clouded her stormy eyes. She was right and wrong. He had to leave because he couldn't control himself. Because the same instincts that rode him hard when he got his hands on her again had been there from the start. He just didn't know what they were at the time.

Mate.

He squinted at the sky and a pair of birds flying

together above the trees. "I don't think I ever really left."

"It sure felt like you did. Every second felt like you were trying to hurt me as much as possible."

"I know. I was." He turned back to her. Hard eyes watched him, but she hugged her knees close to her chest. Vulnerable, and not. She'd changed since they'd been together. Hardened herself, just like he'd tried to do. He thought he'd succeeded until she launched herself back into his life. "I didn't trust myself with you. You were the most precious thing to me, Liv. I'd rather die than make you go through what happened to me. I couldn't stick around and hurt you, but I did it anyway by running without any explanation."

Liv cocked her head to the side. "I want to see your bear."

Alex hesitated. His bear puffed out his chest and fucking preened. "I don't think that's a good idea."

She unfolded from her chair and stepped closer. Her fingers trailed across his collarbone. "I don't think you'll hurt me."

He caught her wrist and forced her back a step. Her tangy scent clogged up his nose and threatened to overwhelm his resistance. "I will," he growled.

Liv shook her head, hair swaying with her dismissal. "You won't. I trust that much."

"But you don't trust me."

"No." She lifted her chin. "Not entirely. Not yet."

"I wanted to bite you, Liv." Then. Now. The last time he had her in his arms. Her choice which she picked. They were all true.

Grey eyes blinked at him and a small smile played out across her features. Her lips twitched, red flushed over her skin. Caution and confusion entered her scent. Her eyes, too, churned with the complicated emotions.

Quietly, she said, "I know what that means."

"Then you know why this is a bad idea. If I lose control…"

"You're still here."

"You haven't told me to leave." He brushed his thumb over her knuckles. So close. He could drag her down into his lap and kiss her senseless.

He'd just wanted to protect her and he fell for her again. Or opened that door in his mind he'd locked her behind. One thing was for certain, he couldn't hold her close and keep himself apart.

Maybe Ethan was right. Maybe he needed to stop fighting and learn to let himself go.

His bear growled, soft and low.

Liv dragged her fingers over his cheek and he leaned into the touch. With her, he didn't feel like he dove headfirst toward the ground. She slowed his fall to a controlled landing.

That was the crack his bear needed. The beast shoved against all his defenses and spilled through on a wave of bad ideas and recklessness.

"Rules, Liv." Alex tucked a finger under her chin and forced a look. "If I tell you to go inside and lock the door, you do it."

She nodded.

Alex pushed to his feet. So close, he brushed against her in more than one spot. Fire licked at him from the inside out.

"Stand still. Don't run. The bear just might give chase." He hauled his shirt over his head. "Last chance, Olivia."

She dipped her chin, eyes fierce. "Show me."

CHAPTER 15

Liv held her breath as Alex stepped away. He tossed the shirt in his hands at her, then went for his boots. Those landed with twin thuds at her feet. Faint, silvery scars crossed over his arms, a few on his chest.

Her fingers dug into his shirt the moment he went for the button of his jeans.

"Hoping for something more, baby?" he asked with a smirk.

"Nothing I haven't seen before," she replied coolly and definitely without a hitch in her voice.

Alex's grin widened and he popped the button. The zipper came next, then he shoved the fabric over his hips. Nothing else existed between him and the whole wide world.

Liv struggled to keep her eyes locked on his face. Tried, and failed.

Once again, she was struck with just how damn good he looked. She had no way to estimate just how much muscle he'd packed on in the six years since they were involved, but she could appreciate the end result. Lines marked the slabs on his stomach and led straight down to the prize jutting from his body. Heat curled down her spine and straight to her core at the sight of his long, thick cock standing at attention.

"I thought you wanted to see my bear," Alex mused, straightening to his full height and lacing his fingers behind his head.

Liv jerked her gaze to his face. Red flushed over her cheeks. Busted. One thousand percent, no salvaging the situation, busted. She crossed her arms over her chest and deflected. "Are you going to shift, or just stand there?"

A growl reached her ears even over the cracks and painful pops. She almost looked away before steeling herself. Alex went through the shift anytime he and his bear switched places. The first time had been agony, he said, and she doubted the rest were picnics in the park. The least she could do was acknowledge the process.

Finally, a huge bear stood in front of her.

The beast was huge. Black fur without an ounce of color covered him.

She took a step forward, but he growled and her foot slid back into place. *Don't run. The bear might give chase.*

That applied to getting nearer, it seemed.

The bear moved. Pure power scratched at the primal side of her brain. She knew Alex was inside there, somewhere, but her instincts still screamed at her to run and hide from the paws that looked bigger than her head. Each claw looked like it'd stretch the length of her hand easily. She'd be a soft target if he chose to use them against her.

He wouldn't, right?

The bear continued his forward momentum and shoved his head into her stomach. Liv stumbled back a step. The bear jerked his attention to her, small growl rattling in his throat and worry lighting up his glowing eyes, but she only laughed.

"You're stronger than I expected," she explained.

Slowly, she reached forward and stroked an ear. Soft fur passed between her fingers before he shook his head and moved out of her grasp. "Ticklish?"

Alex huffed.

He continued to move around her. Slowly, she

relaxed. Liv trailed a hand down his back and over his sides. She pressed a palm against his shoulder and felt the muscles underneath bunch and contract with each step. But he was the one taking a spin around her and she felt just as scrutinized as the attention she gave him.

This was Alex. Monster under his skin, but still a playful scoundrel. Mouthy fighter who just didn't know when to quit.

She understood why he left. The pain still stung, but not as bad as before. She couldn't imagine turning into such a creature with no prior knowledge. Then to contend with all the senses and urges that came with the animal?

Strong man. Impressive. Asshole, but one she felt pride for. He didn't let that incident destroy him. He fought to stay on his feet. That she wasn't a witness didn't negate the accomplishment.

"You survived," she murmured with pride.

His growl turned ragged and choked. His shape shimmered as he changed back from beast to man.

Then he was on two feet and striding right for her.

"Alex." His name was the only word she managed to speak before his mouth collided with her own. The shocked gasp turned into a harsh kiss of tangling tongues and biting teeth. Wild, just like him. Just like his bear.

That kiss was his apology for everything. For hurting her in the past. For throwing up walls at every turn. They still had miles to go, but there was a whisper of hope on his tongue and in the fingers he tangled in her hair. She wanted to believe, not just in him, but in them together.

Alex pulled back, but only barely. Their breath mingled as they both sucked down air. "Invite me inside, Liv," he said in a low, gravelly voice. "I need to hear you say it."

She thought of making some crack about him being a secret vampire-bear hybrid and discarded it immediately. Her blood pumped loud and fast. Her heart and stomach and head and every inch of her demanded to feel more of the sexy, naked man holding her close. Jokes were for later when the hard edge of desperation was worn down.

She took a step backward, tugging him as she went. "Alex. Come inside with me. I need this."

She didn't make it more than three steps inside before the door slammed shut and his hands landed on her hips. He dragged her close to his body and just like last time, she could feel every inch of his chiseled frame pressing against her. Her skin crackled with energy, nerve endings zinging as his hands seemed to touch her everywhere all at once. Liv threw an arm over his shoulder just as he bit down on her neck.

Alex walked her forward, then spun her around and lifted her to the counter.

The air felt heavy around him and she had to work to inhale her next breath. Worth it, because his delicious earthy and manly scent was strong enough to almost taste. Liv leaned forward and pressed her lips to his collarbone.

The growl in his throat stilled her. The feel of it vibrated right to her middle. She wanted more. More of that noise, more of his hands on her body, more teeth and snarls and glowing eyes.

More him.

Liv drew a ragged breath and on her exhale, his mouth found hers for another hungry kiss.

She worked shaky fingers down the front of her blouse. When the last one came undone, Alex shoved the sides apart. He stripped her of her shirt and bra in what felt like a microsecond.

His hands skimmed up her sides and cupped her breasts, hot fingers deftly rolling her nipples between his fingers. Liv arched into him when he bent to lick and suck first one breast, then the other.

He left a trail of hot desire across her skin. Over her breasts, down her ribs. He circled her navel and teased under the waist of her slacks. She was a keening, mewling mess by the time he worked them open and helped her shimmy free.

"Fuck, Liv," he growled and dropped to his knees. He swept his eyes from her toes to her face, then settled right at her middle. He licked his lips. "Been wanting to do this."

He bent his head. His tongue gently caressed her. Decadent delight shivered down her spine and Liv moaned. She planted her hands on the counter to ground her to something as she watched Alex's move between her thighs.

Then his fingers slid inside her. She held her breath for a second. Another. He rolled his eyes up to hers, the green churning with the glow of his inner beast.

He wasn't running.

The slow deliberation of his pumping fingers built pressure inside her. She couldn't ignore the fire or waste any energy on what ifs or events of the past. They were there, now, and he strung her pleasure out like he was born to it. The years between them were knocked away, the dust cleared, and he touched her the way she needed.

He overwhelmed her. Made her head spin. His fingers pumped into her again and again, while his tongue licked and sucked and stroked her. Alex didn't tease. He mercilessly, completely owned her.

His ownership came with a price: her utter pleasure.

His groans mingled and mixed with her soft cries and breathy gasps. The world melted away. There was no kitchen with a coffee mug in the sink. No living room at her back. No window overlooking the back yard, hell, no back yard to speak of. There was only Alex and his fingers and tongue.

Her stomach hollowed on her sharp breaths and her vision darkened at the edges. Liv's fingers tingled and her toes curled. Right there, right on the edge, she knew the moment was important. As important as the man giving it to her.

Liv cried out and twisted her fingers in his hair. She rode the wave of pure bliss as he brought her steadily back down to reality.

Low growl rumbling in his chest, Alex eased his fingers out of her and licked them clean. Glowing green eyes filled with utter male smugness as he rolled back to his feet.

He settled between her thighs again, thick cock

resting right at her entrance. Liv swallowed back her desperate pant of need.

"I've missed hearing you come," he said against the shell of her ear. "You don't know how many times just thinking about it has gotten me off."

She took two tries to make her voice work. "You've thought about me?" Warmth filled her core at the idea.

Alex nipped at her earlobe. "Hard to forget perfection."

Liv lost her retort when he swiped his thumb against her clit. Her body jolted in response, liquid heat rushing to meet whatever he'd do to her next.

PERFECTION. He'd said the word. It echoed and rattled around in his head, bouncing from one corner of his mind to the other. His bear rumbled his agreement and his displeasure.

Alex buried his nose into the crook of Liv's neck and eased his fingers back into her. Her silky smooth muscles tightened around him. Her breath sounded loud in his ears and his cock twitched in response.

Perfection. He meant every fucking syllable.

But his bear wanted more. Needed more. The

tiny bite he'd given her before when he lost control wasn't a complete bond. His scent was under her skin, but it'd fade away in days. Then anyone brave enough to try could swoop in and not know she belonged to him.

He had to make that connection complete. His gums ached with the press of fangs.

Alex froze mid-stroke.

He couldn't tie her to him. Not now. Maybe not ever. He'd survived, just like she said. But surviving was different from living. He was on a path with no future and no mate. He had to fix himself and all the shit that followed him before he could bond her to him.

His bear slashed at his insides and raged over the denial of their mate. She was right there, ready and willing. He just had to take—

No. No taking. Not from Liv. He couldn't hurt her. Biting would be hurting. She didn't know his world as well as she thought. She'd leave if he misbehaved, and neither he nor the bear wanted that. They needed her. Wanted to protect her. There was no doing that if she was mated without understanding everything.

His bear roared, but the press of fangs faded to something manageable.

"Move," Liv ordered on a low groan.

So he did. He wrapped her legs around his waist and twisted to pin her to the nearest wall with one hand above her head.

Gorgeous woman. Sexy as hell. And stretched out all for him.

Short black hair framed her face. The rosy color on her cheeks spread down her neck, more prominent where his teeth had grazed her skin. Her scent filled his nose, sank into his lungs, and threatened to drown him. At least he'd die a happy man.

She leaned forward and nipped his lip. "I swear to all that's holy, if you leave me with blue balls again—"

Fuck, she was everything.

Alex cut her off with a roll of his hips. Wet heat coated his length. The teeth she'd used on him caught her lower lip in a strangled cry.

She threw her head back, but her eyes stayed locked on him. Emotion swirled in the stormy grey. So expressive. So damn beautiful.

He needed to see the hurt be replaced with anything else.

Glassy, hot need would do just fine.

He held her spread open and slid back enough to ease his way inside her in slow, controlled thrusts.

Her fingernails dragged over his shoulders and down his chest. The soft, greedy pants of breath heaving in her chest only encouraged him more. He wanted her desperate, and holy fuck, she was right there.

Alex slid home the last inch with a strangled groan. He leaned his forehead against Liv's, their eyes meeting and breath mingling. Her inner muscles fluttered around him as she adjusted to his size. Fuck, it was hard to stay still. He wanted to slam into her again and again until he felt her grip him as tightly as she'd done his fingers.

When he moved, stars exploded behind his eyelids and his bear roared with victory. Liv clamped down around him, taking every inch of his cock, clawing and clinging to him just like he remembered.

No. Better than he remembered. Because she was really there.

He pressed his nose into the crook of her neck and licked her slick skin. "That's it, Liv. Strangle my dick. Want to know how good this is for you."

"Too long," she panted.

Alex thrust into her again, harder. She whimpered and writhed in his hands. "Too long since someone fucked you the way you need to be fucked?"

Her answer was lost on a sharp breath as he bucked into her. He slid a hand between their bodies and stroked her clit, loving the way she threw her head back and moaned. For him. All for him and what he did to her.

"I pictured this so many times. Imagined how you sounded and felt." He pressed his mouth to her throat. Her heart beat under his lips, urging him faster.

"Here now," she whimpered.

Fucking right. His fantasy had come to life.

Alex groaned with every savage thrust. His balls drew up high and tight as Liv fluttered around him. Red spread over her cheeks and down her chest. Her eyes were hot and hungry when she rolled them open to peek at him. Those delicious little glances were almost his undoing as much as Liv herself.

Her heart thundered in her chest. Even over their grunts and groans, their mingled cries, he could hear her beating like a drum. Alex drove into her again, harder. Faster. Until he lost himself in the sensations spiraling off Liv and her panting, incoherent babble. Then she tensed, her hips rolling against him and her mouth dropping open for the one final, perfect cry.

"Fuck," he hissed, every cell in his body demanding that final connection as she exploded around him. Alex ground his teeth together to keep from letting go and claiming her. He thrust into her once, twice more, holding deep and spilling warmth in a release that stole his breath.

Liv nodded. After a moment of standing with their foreheads pressed together and breath mingling, Liv pressed his fingertips to the hollow of his throat.

"You're purring," she said softly.

"Don't be ridiculous," Alex huffed. "Bears don't purr."

"Maybe bears don't. But *you* do." She kissed the corner of his mouth. "It's cute."

"I'm a bear. Ferocious. Not cute."

"Except for your fluffy, ticklish ears."

Alex growled and pulled away from the wall. Quick steps took him into her bedroom. He laid her gently on the bed and followed her down, not wanting to break their connection. Her soft laugh turned to a pleased sigh.

"No more talk about my fluffy ears or purrs," he mouthed against her neck.

Liv wound her arms around his neck and drew him closer. Her legs wrapped around him again and her eyes heated. "Only if you're staying."

Alex grinned against her skin. "Made the mistake of leaving before. Don't want a repeat."

His heart unlocked. Melted. What-fucking-ever. He'd spent six fucking years without the taste of her on his tongue or the feel of her in his arms.

One single truth branded itself across his mind.

He couldn't lose her again.

CHAPTER 16

Liv rummaged in her purse. No key. She checked through her wallet and all the pockets and still came up empty. A peek through the lab windows showed no one else had arrived for the day. Balls.

She retraced her steps from the night before. She'd swiped herself out of the office portion of the team's area, then stuffed her key into the same pocket as always. She and Jenny took the elevator together and put both their bags through the security search. Jenny handed Liv her bag and then they went their separate ways.

The elevator dinged and Liv turned. Leela and Jenny both stepped out with broad smiles.

"Morning," they greeted at the same time.

"You stuck?" Leela asked.

It must have slipped out when she tossed her purse to a table when Alex surprised her. It hadn't been the only thing hastily scooped up and placed elsewhere. An entire load of laundry was dumped back in the basket and stuffed into her closet before she met him outside.

"Forgot my damn pass at the cabin this morning," Liv said before her brain continued that train of thought.

Jenny grinned. "Something else on your mind?"

"I don't know what you mean."

Leela snickered. "Our little neighborhood is a small town within a small town. It's hard not to notice a big truck parked outside a cabin."

Well, the cat was out of the bag. Or bear.

"We need details," Jenny demanded as she swiped her card in the door.

"It was..." Great. Wonderful. Abso-fucking-lutely amazing. She doubted she'd had as many orgasms in a single night. All the dirty rumors about shifter virility were true. Alex had been insatiable.

Even beyond that, the entire night tugged at her heartstrings. She wasn't naive enough to believe they'd picked up right where they left off, but there was something to be said about intimacy with someone she knew. They were already past the trial-and-error stage and well into knowing how and where to touch. All those little unspoken cues were acted upon and made everything that much better.

Heat simmered in her core. Alex had kissed her goodbye that morning before making dirty promises to have her coming again before dinner. Her mouth dried at the memory of his deep voice whispering in her ear as he drew another release from her body.

"It was unexpected," she said at last.

That was the truth. The night was unexpected, and she didn't know what to expect from the future. Sleeping together didn't change the past. He'd made his apologies for hurting her and gave his reasoning. His damage was still on display. Knowing a rogue attacked him and still tortured him from afar wasn't something she knew how to navigate. He had six years to come to terms with it and hadn't. She was still stuck on processing the information.

Jenny waved a hand in front of her face. "And she's back. Unexpected, my ass. Wipe the drool off your chin, Liv."

"And for that, no details for you." Liv strode straight for her desk, struggling to keep her shoulders from shaking with a laugh.

"Prude!" Jenny called after her.

The rest of the team slowly filtered in and started their day. Coffee and snacks were brought to desks for polite chatting and checking for any messages that may have come in overnight. Once they were settled, Dr. Franco called them together for a quick morning meeting to plan out the rest of their day. Results were highlighted and assignments given, then they were dismissed to continue working on their projects.

Liv had just settled into a workstation in the lab area when the doors buzzed for a new entry. Dr. Rylee Strathorn entered the office space and made a beeline right for Dr. Franco's office. Outside the doors, two big-shouldered security guards waited. Everyone glanced up at once before ducking their eyes back down in mock dismissal.

Just a few minutes later, both Dr. Strathorn and Dr. Franco entered the lab with seriousness written across their faces. Rylee looked around the room and settled a stern look on Liv.

"Liv, can you come with me, please?"

Liv pushed to her feet. No one said a word, but the back of her neck prickled with all the eyes focused on her. She felt like she was twelve and had been called to the principal's office instead of an

adult with a degree and a place on a highly presti-
gious team of scientists.

Together, they walked out into the hall. Liv
jumped when the security guards fell into step
behind them. "What's this about?" she asked once
they reached the elevator.

Rylee glanced in her direction before looking
straight ahead and pressed the floor number.
"There's been another leak," she answered in a
clipped tone.

Liv's heart pounded. Another leak, and she was
pulled from the lab for questioning. She fought the
urge to stuff her hands in her pockets to keep them
from shaking. Better to let them hang free than hide
them away and look guilty. She'd done nothing
wrong.

She followed Rylee out of the elevator and
straight into her office with security right on their
heels.

"I'm sorry to do this, but prompt action is needed." Rylee rubbed at her temples the moment she
settled into her desk. "Sometimes I wish I could just
give this all up and find a space in the labs."

Liv glanced over her shoulder. The men didn't hold
any weapons she could see, but she didn't doubt they

could have her knocked to the floor in half a second if they deemed her a threat. Their presence set her nerves on edge. "I'm still a little confused why I'm here."

"There was a leak last night," Rylee repeated. "A data dump traced back to our servers. As you know, we've put extra security measures in place to detect any unusual activity."

"Precautions. I understand."

"Then you'll understand when I ask what you were doing logging in last night at," she glanced at the paperwork, "9:56."

Liv stared at her for a long second before comprehending the words. Not just words. Accusation. "I didn't." A little more forcefully, she added, "I had company over. You can ask him. I wasn't out of sight at any moment long enough to pull off any espionage."

"His name?"

"Alex Carter." Well, the bear was out of the bag again.

Rylee's eyebrows rose, but she only asked, "What time did he arrive at your place?"

"He was waiting for me when I got home."

"Did he have access to your key card or laptop at any time?"

"No. Believe me, Alex is not the leak." Liv leaned

forward, lips pursing. "My pass was missing this morning, though. I thought I'd misplaced it, but maybe it was taken by whoever did this."

Behind her, the security officers shifted where they stood. "You can ask Jenny and Leela, they let me into the lab today."

Rylee shot a look over her head. "Take me through your timeline yesterday. Let's see if we can pinpoint what happened."

"I came to work and logged in, per policy." Liv watched Rylee's finger trail down the page. Her card access and computer codes were documented anytime she used them. "Lunch out, then lunch back in. That'd have been around noon and one. Then I left with everyone else. Jenny and I rode the elevator down together."

"And sometime between leaving last night and this morning, your pass went missing."

"That's right."

Rylee made a star next to one line. "Has anyone on your team been acting strangely, in your opinion? This is purely confidential, of course."

Liv thought for a moment then shook her head. "I can't really say. I've only been here for a few weeks. My baseline for normal could be someone's overall weird."

Rylee stepped back from her desk and followed one of the security guards into the hallway. Liv's lungs refused to work while the two conferred. She held tightly to the fact that she'd done nothing remotely like stealing information. The accusation stung. She couldn't be blamed for something she didn't do.

She hoped.

The longer she was left alone with the one security guard, though, the more she began to doubt. Worry slithered through her head and slicked her palms. Maybe there was just too much evidence against her. Someone thought her a useful tool to meet their nefarious goal. All she had in her defense was her word.

Finally, the door opened again and Rylee stepped back through. Time slowed to a crawl as Rylee crossed the room.

This was it. No more dream job.

Liv prepared to throw herself at Rylee's mercy. She'd fight for a second chance. If that failed, she'd beg for mercy. Anything but being thrown out of the facility.

Rylee favored her with a gracious smile. "Thanks for coming down, Liv. I recommend you head straight to the security office and get your pass replaced."

Liv opened and closed her mouth twice as the words filtered through her brain. She sank back in her chair. Relief flooded her veins and made her head swim. "That's it?" she blurted.

"I had my doubts since these troubles started before you arrived. These gentlemen here say they can't smell any lie. You're free to go back to the office and we'll continue our investigation."

She didn't need to be told twice. She also didn't want any other questions fired her way and raising any doubts. She'd been given a reprieve, and she freaking took it.

Once she made it back to the lab—new key card and computer passcode in hand—she successfully fobbed off questions about some forgotten paperwork. The entire line of questioning put her on the outside all over again.

She wasn't just the newbie on the team. Someone targeted her to cover up their crimes. She didn't even know if it was someone in the room with her at that moment, but the odds pointed in that direction.

Liv plugged in her earbuds, cranked up the volume of her music, and threw herself spitefully into her work. She wouldn't be someone's patsy. The thought of it made her furious. She'd worked her ass off in college and every single job she'd had after to prove her worth in the science world. Blaming her for leaking information stripped away all her accomplishments and credibility. It was a career ender.

Carefully handling samples when she wanted to slam down trays and cause a fuss, Liv loaded up a slide in the microscope as part of a routine check.

She and everyone else on the team collected samples from bitten shifters in Bearden and from satellite locations. Those samples were split and edited, then introduced back together. The new material was given time to work, hopefully with great results. Most edits were busts and showed little to no changes. Others had scary results and wiped out the entire sample. All required monitoring and copious notes.

But this one...

"Guys, come look," Liv urged.

"You got something?" Barry asked from his station.

Liv peeked again. She hadn't imagined a thing. "Yeah. I got something."

Bitten shifter blood cells had ridges all around like some jagged castle wall. Normal human cells and born shifters didn't have those markers. That'd been the major clue that perhaps there was something on the genetic level that could be changed.

The cells she looked at came from a bitten shifter, but none of the ridges were present.

Liv stepped back as Matt took the first look. When he made room, Barry took his place. Soon they'd all taken double and triple looks.

Questions fired her way. What she'd deleted, added, manipulated. Length of time she'd let the sample rest. Age of the sample before she processed it, how long the donor had been a shifter. They grilled her about every last detail in their excitement before scattering and demanding she upload her findings for their own continued experiments.

They were so far from successfully reversing a change, but Liv couldn't help but feel a little proud. For those like Alex who'd been unwillingly turned into a shifter, help was on the horizon. Hopefully.

But a single doubt cooled her excitement.

One member of the team worked to put the information in the wrong hands.

CHAPTER 17

Alex wiped a hand across his forehead and settled his Stetson. The days were growing warmer as spring marched toward summer. The heat usually irritated his bear—another item on a very long list—but there was hardly a rumble from the beast as he leaned against the fence and watched Daisy try to force one of the barn cats to play.

No, the bear had been content all damn week. Liv did that to him. A balm on his soul. Sandpaper over his rough edges. Every night with her was better than the last. He'd only gotten into seven fights since she took him to her bed, which had to be some sort of record. That alone was a reason to keep her around, even if he didn't already have purely selfish desires to do so.

Heat flared in the base of his spine. His bear flashed a lazy sending of Liv with a mate mark on her skin.

Alex scowled and shoved the beast aside. He knew what the bear wanted. Hell, he wanted it, too. But those wants didn't change who he was or how he was made. Mating her wasn't an option. Not yet.

Not with his monster still drawing breath in the world.

Not until she could truly forgive him for hurting her.

Not until he could get himself under control.

He squeezed his eyes closed and pressed back on the rolling irritation from his other side.

Behind him, the door to the main house banged open. Last in and first out was usually how he handled lunch and it seemed the rest of the clan were finishing up. An afternoon of work still needed to be done before he could taste Liv again. He craved her like air and water and everything else needed to keep him alive.

Ethan approached, polishing off the remains of a final sandwich Tansey had provided the clan for lunch. Without preamble, he launched into new orders. "I need you to take over on the trail today."

Alex jerked upright. "Hell no."

Ethan spread his hands wide. "Hunter and Joss are still at the midwife's. There's a hole in the fence from the damn lion pride brawling again that needs closing before the herds start mixing."

"So I'll finish up here and go mend the fence."

"After the amazing time you had on your last ride? I wouldn't want you to miss it."

"Ethan."

"I should have thrown you in the deep end long ago." Ethan fixed him with a flat look. "It's an hour here on the ranch. A small group of two families. This should be easy."

He wanted to snarl and deny the assignment. Give way to his bear and run off for the rest of the day. But that wasn't what someone steady would do. For Liv, he had to grit his teeth and make himself work. She wanted kids one day—if she hadn't changed her mind from before they fell apart—and he couldn't be a father if he snapped at every little thing.

His bear immediately settled with the bonus of flashed sendings featuring tiny, dark-haired monsters running around his and Liv's feet. An entire pack of them.

Alex let go of a held breath and forced his shoulders to relax. "Fine," he agreed.

He could be better. For Liv.

"Good." Ethan punched him on the shoulder. "Because it sounds like we have some early arrivals."

Alex cocked his head and swore. Sure enough, the sound of a car bumping up the road reached his ears. "You owe me for this," he grumbled.

Ethan flicked him off over his shoulder as he strode toward the barn. "Yeah, your regular paycheck!"

Alex steeled himself as the car pulled to a stop. A family of three exited the vehicle—mother, father, and a boy who couldn't have been more than six or seven. Alex didn't know for sure. Judging ages was never his talent.

The kid's excitement was clearly written all over his face and scent. He stared with wide eyes at the house, the barn, and him and Jesse. He'd even dressed as a miniature cowboy, complete with hat and boots.

The kid tugged on the hem of his mother's shirt. "Where's Lula?" he asked in a whisper loud enough for even a human to hear across the yard.

"Patience, Gabe," his mother answered. "They haven't even started yet. We got here early."

Jesse went to tend to them, but Alex reached the group first. He nodded to the other man and Jesse backed off. After a long second and a hard-eyed look.

"Early enough to help out. I'm Alex." Alex winked at the parents and knelt in front of Gabe. "You must be Gabe. I heard you asked especially to meet Lula."

The young boy nodded and planted his hands on his hips. "Does she really like long stalks of hay?"

Alex held back an affectionate curse for Tansey. Instead, he reached forward and adjusted the brim of Gabe's cowboy hat. "She sure does. The longer the better. Why don't we rustle some up and you can give it to her before we head out?"

The boy practically beamed. With a nod from his parents, Alex led him into the barn.

"Wait here," he told the kid. He dipped into the feed room and returned with a small handful of hay which he passed over to Gabe. He bounced on his toes as Alex opened the stall door and led Lula out.

"Keep your hand flat and hold it out. There you go, she knows what she's looking for." Gabe's loud squeal pierced his ears, and he hunched his shoulders. A couple of the other horses jerked their heads at the noise, but Lula stayed focused on the snack in the boy's hand.

"Now, since you're here early, you have to put in some work with us adults. Got it?"

Gabe nodded, smelling serious even with his eyes as wide as saucers.

Alex went through the routine with the kid. He even found him a stepstool to better reach Lula with the brush. After he went over everywhere Gabe brushed to be sure Lula had the proper treatment needed, he showed the kid how to throw on a blanket, then the saddle. Gabe laughed at Lula sucking in a big breath to keep the straps nice and loose, and again at needing to walk her a few steps to trick her into breathing again.

By the time Lula was properly cinched up, and the stirrups shortened to an approximate length for a child, Jesse had brushed down and prepped nearly all the other horses. Alex expected him to be irritated at the extra work, but he only smelled amused.

Soon enough, the second family arrived. The parents and one very moody teenager joined the party. Then they were off, with Gabe clinging to his side like a burr.

The kid was relentless with his questions. Every shrub they passed or hill they mounted, he wanted to know if there had been any cowboy battles in that exact spot. When they passed by the herd of cattle, he asked how many were on the ranch, if they all made milk, and if Alex would let him ride a bucking bull. The last sparked another question and Gabe desperately needed to know if Lula would buck him off into a pit of rattlesnakes.

Alex glanced over his shoulder. Gabe's parents watched the scenery with contented expressions, probably thankful they weren't in firing range for the endless number of questions the boy plucked out of his head.

Telling the boy they raised beef cattle instead of milk stock and reassuring him that no rattlesnake pits were on the ranch was easier than dealing with a group of scientists and Liv's scent distracting him. Alex darkened as the other invading scent of that trip scalded his memory. His bear rumbled protectively. For Liv and for the innocent, incessant kid at his side.

But that rise in his bear didn't last long. The beast settled back down with a huff, but he remained on high alert.

Something had shifted in the animal. Instead of the unhinged fury and need to fight, there was a new focus. An end goal. Something to live and die for, even.

Alex could have sworn he was losing his voice by the time the group rode back up to the barn. Daisy greeted them with a long, drawn-out moo that set Gabe into a fit of giggles.

Still feeling steady, Alex jerked his head toward the small paddock once they were all dismounted. "Want to meet her?"

Gabe twisted to his parents. "Can I?"

"If he says it's safe," his father said.

"Go on," Jesse said. "I'll start settling the horses."

"Stay here," he told Gabe at the fence. "She can get a little excited sometimes."

Alex slipped through the wood slats. Daisy spotted him and immediately ran toward him, ramming her head into his side. She nudged him hard again and admonished him with another loud moo. Gabe cackled and clapped his hands.

He managed to lure the calf back to the fence where she stuck her face through the slats. "This is Daisy," he introduced. "Daisy, meet Gabe."

The calf slurped the boy with a long, sloppy lick. "I'm not a lollipop, you silly moocow!" he giggled.

Alex snorted and crossed the fence again.

"Thank you so much for the wonderful time," Gabe's mother said. "Gabe has been talking about this trip for weeks."

"Glad we didn't disappoint." Alex touched fingers to the brim of his Stetson.

Jesse appeared at their sides. "I have some sanitizer for those slobbery hands."

Alex's bear rumbled as he grabbed one of the horses still needing to be settled and entered the barn. The words didn't taste like a lie. Hell, he even felt proud of himself. He'd kept his cool and let some kid crawl all over the place and have a good afternoon.

Maybe, just fucking maybe, he had a shot at getting his life together.

Inside, Hunter stared at him with wide-eyed shock. Lorne wasn't far off from the expression, either. Ethan looked as proud as a damn peacock.

"What?" Alex growled at him.

"Who the fuck are you?" Hunter asked. He slowly circled him, then poked him hard in the chest. "You're real, whatever you are."

"Maybe a robot, then?" Jesse suggested when he entered with another horse.

Lorne shook his head. "I still vote on body snatcher."

"Fuck you all." Alex raised both his middle fingers.

Ethan chuckled. "There he is."

The work of closing down the trail ride went quickly with everyone helping. Once done, he ran a hand through his hair. Fuck, he needed a haircut. A real one, not the choppy kind he did in his own mirror. The idea of sitting still while someone chatted at him was still too far off.

Maybe soon. For Liv.

"I'm going to wash up and head out," he announced.

"Got somewhere to be?" Ethan asked innocently.

"Someone to see, more like," Hunter answered with an obscene rocking of his hips.

Liv. The thought of seeing her again made his heart pound and his dick hard. Yeah, it wasn't the sunshine and butterflies and rainbows girls talked about, but that was as close as he'd get to admitting his excitement. Especially around a bunch of other men who were as likely to punch him as to push their sappiness on him.

Alex grinned. "Least I'll be getting more than shitty diapers here soon."

"Implying you're already dealing with shitty diapers. I knew you were an ass, but you didn't need to tell us about your hole problems. Poor Liv."

"Fuck off," Alex laughed. He flicked them off again and strode out of the barn and toward his hut.

For the first time oh, six years, he felt light. Like he could do anything. He wasn't stuck being the asshole of the clan. He had more ahead of him than Ethan putting him down. He could be fixed.

The scent hit him full in the face as soon as he stepped on his porch. Alex whipped around and stared down the road.

His lip lifted in a silent snarl. Motherfucker. His monster had tracked him all the way to his front door.

Alex stalked back toward his home, ready to tear into the asshole and exact his revenge for the messy years spent apart from Liv. He stilled the moment he squared up to his front door.

Right at eye level, a picture of Liv dangled from a small knife driven into the wood.

Alex whirled with a roar. His bear lunged forward and tore through his control, ripping out of him in a painful instant.

The others came running, but he was already too far gone. All the jagged edges Liv smoothed down pierced him at once.

Blood. He wanted blood and death. That rogue bastard, preferably. Anything else with a pulse would do.

Ethan reached him first, twin paws knocking him left and right. Lorne nipped at his back end and he whirled, snapping his jaws inches from the other bear. Jesse baited him back around again.

Four on one, and he was stuck in the middle.

Fuck that. He didn't care. He bit and clawed and tore and snapped. He needed the taste of blood on his tongue. Needed to feel flesh give way under his blows. The fight was the only thing that satisfied his beast.

And when he started to slow and couldn't hit back as fast, he still didn't give up. He couldn't let them win. Bowing down to them was the same as letting that bastard maul him all over again.

Ethan peeled away, leaving the other three to pace just out of range. His alpha's shape shimmered as fur melted back into skin. Then the man stood in place of the bear.

"Easy," Ethan said in a low voice. His chest rose and fell in heavy breaths. "Steady."

Alex pawed at the ground and huffed. Fire still burned through his veins. Blood steadily dripped from cuts all over his body.

He still wouldn't give up.

"Shift back."

Alex snarled. Ethan's eyes filled with pity, which just made him even angrier.

"Shift," his alpha ordered with all the power he could muster.

Alex roared as his bear was kicked to the back of his head. The painful, forced change left him on hands and knees in the dirt, sweat streaming down his face. He lifted his head just enough to glare murder at his alpha.

Ethan slashed a look to the others. "Go," he ordered. "Find how he got all the way up here without anyone noticing and where's he's gone."

In a flash, the bears scattered with their noses to the ground. They kept a wide berth from Alex, but edged close enough to his home to gather what fresh evidence they could before chasing down a ghost.

"I did what you said," Alex panted. "I stopped fighting for one damn minute and that bastard leaves his mark."

"I know," Ethan answered.

The man knelt next to him, but didn't touch him. He was too raw for anything physical. But the near presence of his alpha offered a tiny bit of calm.

Calm he immediately rejected.

A snarl built up inside him. The noise echoed in all the dark places that had hardened over the years. Solid pain, now calcified. He dug his fingers into the dirt. "I can't do this. I can't have her and him exist together."

"You can and you will. You have to grab hold of the good before the bad eats you alive. That's the only way to survive."

"There's no surviving this." The words tasted like ashes.

"That's where you're wrong," Ethan said quietly. "You made it this far. You might be limping and hurting right now, but you're a stubborn sonovabitch. You think the others could go through having their lives reduced to rubble and make it out on the other side? You think *I* could? You'll survive because you don't know when to give up."

Alex laughed mirthlessly. "I'm giving up right now. Just fucking put me down already."

"You know that bastard's next stop will be your mate's. Is that what you want for her?"

He shook his head, hard. His bear rushed to the surface, ready to fight again even after being forced back. Alex locked his elbows to keep from falling face first in the dirt.

He knew what it was like to lose his humanity. Those awful, confusing hours where he wasn't sure if he was dead or alive or somewhere in between weren't anything he wanted Liv to experience. The loss of control, the thoughts that weren't his own. Rubble. Ethan saw his world as rubble, but that was too generous. Rubble still had forms and shapes. His world had been reduced to ash. Nothing was left without Liv.

"Then you'll keep going. Keep fighting. Don't give up. You can't let him win."

Alex sucked down a shaky breath, then another. He rolled his eyes up and met Ethan's. "For Liv."

His alpha nodded. "For Liv. And for a giant fuck you to the asshole who did this to you."

CHAPTER 18

Liv listened for the sound of a truck pulling to a stop outside her door. Her stomach fluttered despite her best efforts to keep calm and cool. There was no reason to get all giddy or worse, give in to her worries.

Except she was about to go on her first public-outing-slash-date with Alex in six years.

Part of her was convinced he wouldn't show. The other part of her didn't know what to do if he did.

He'd disappointed her the night before when he called to say he wouldn't be joining her for dinner. In the same breath, he promised to make it up to her the next morning. She'd agreed, but she couldn't get the rough rasp of his voice out of her head.

Liv pressed a hand to her stomach when the

rumbling sound of an engine rolled to a stop and then died. She squeezed her eyes closed as a door creaked open, then slammed closed again. Loud steps clunked over her porch and after a moment, knuckles rapped against her door.

Alex had shown up.

To practically anyone else in the world, the action wasn't a big deal. It felt huge to Liv. He'd left her before without an explanation, but he was here, now, trying to figure out how they fit together.

Mate.

Nope. She shut the door on that thought. His bear was drawn to her. He'd admitted as much when he said he wanted to bite her. But the rest of it? Mating marks and claiming for all eternity? The man himself? That was all too serious when she still wasn't sure how much she could trust him.

She stared at the door like a crazy person while Alex waited on the other side. Liv shook herself and flung open the door.

"Hey," she greeted the drop dead gorgeous cowboy framing her doorway.

He'd traded a button down for a plain charcoal grey t-shirt and his work boots for hiking shoes. The dark wash jeans were still the same and still clung to his muscled legs in ways that made her core clench and her mouth dry.

Alex leaned in for a quick kiss on her cheek. "Sorry about last night. Emergency on the ranch."

Something in his voice made her shelve her hormones and take a step back. "Is everything okay?"

"It will be," he answered with fierce determination.

Liv pursed her lips, but didn't say anything else. His reaction felt out of place for something that seemed so mundane. But what did she know? He obviously had an attachment to the calves he hand reared. Maybe he had a rough night with a new arrival. He'd certainly been sparse on the details.

She tugged at the thread of doubt that wrapped around her throat and tightened.

"So what's this super secret plan you claimed to have?"

Alex beamed a smile in her direction, but there was still a moment of hesitation. His eyes, too, didn't quite match up to his expression. They were too cold, his eyebrows too drawn, to be naturally happy.

"We're going to the waterfall. It's a small hike. I figured we could have breakfast there before everyone else starts to crowd the place."

"You made me breakfast."

He scoffed and placed a hand over his heart, clearly wounded in the fakest fashion. "Don't sound so doubtful. I taught you how to grill, remember."

Before she could answer, he marched for his truck. He popped open the door and crooked a finger for her to follow. Liv shut her front door. By the time she stepped up next to him, he had a picnic basket on the seat with the lid open for her inspection. Inside was utterly packed with a variety of snacks and finger foods. The crowning glory, however, were the twin bottles of orange juice and champagne.

"Are you trying to get me day drunk, sir?"

"Oh, those? Those are all for me, ma'am. Why do you think I invited you along? You're my designated driver."

The joking eased her tension. "If that's all I am, I guess I'll just stay here."

Alex moved swiftly and pressed her against the side of his truck. He cupped her cheeks and dipped his face to hers. Liv's breath caught in the back of her throat as Alex leaned into her. He slowly sipped at her lips, fingers stroking over her cheeks. He pressed against her in all the right places, heating her from the inside out. Tease of a man didn't change the pace or trail his hands anywhere else, but his kisses alone set her on fire.

"You're so much more than that," he breathed against her lips.

The flutters in her stomach returned with enough force she was surprised her feet stayed on the ground.

"Get in," he said and stepped away. The gravelly sound of his voice sounded like music to her ears. She wasn't alone in feeling the power of that kiss.

The ride to his mystery destination was quiet. At first, Liv thought Alex was just lost in whatever had kept him from visiting her. But the numerous looks he directed at his mirrors hinted at some other trouble.

"Are we being followed?" she asked, twisting in her seat to look behind them.

"No," he answered, much too fast and gruff. The hair on the back of Liv's neck rose. "Just making sure we won't have any interlopers. Tansey threatened to join us."

She relaxed with a huffed laugh. "Threatened, huh? And the big, bad bear is worried about that?"

He slashed a stern look in her direction. "Don't let her fool you. She's not as sweet as she seems."

"So she's yelled at you for being an asshole?"

Alex scowled into the rearview mirror.

Liv laughed again as he made another turn into a park area. She sat up as the road turned to gravel. A sign advertised different hiking trails and a waterfall with convenient arrows pointing sightseers in the right direction.

A blast for fresh air hit all her senses as soon as she hopped out of the truck. Alex narrowed his eyes halfway around the hood, but she just shrugged. She could open doors herself. Besides, he made up for it by hauling the picnic basket.

Alex glanced over his shoulder, then back to her. His scowl immediately changed to a crooked smile. "Ready?"

"Are you sure you're okay?" She scuffed a foot in the gravel. He'd used Tansey as an excuse, but his mind still seemed elsewhere. "We can do this another time. Or go back to my place and just watch a movie."

"No." He shook his head forcefully. "I can't stay cooped up today. I need to burn off some energy."

"Is that you or your bear talking?"

She meant it as a joke, but he turned stone cold serious. "We're one and the same, Liv. You need to understand that."

"I do. As much as someone can who's standing on the outside." The statement wasn't one she expected from someone who'd signed up to possibly rid himself of his inner animal.

She stashed that bit of information away as he twined their fingers together and led her down one trail.

Nature had always been Alex's element. Even when they first met, he was outside every chance he got. Hiking and camping, playing pickup games of dumb sports with other guys on campus, even choosing to study under natural light and inhaling fresh air. Liv expected Alex to relax as they walked further down the trail. Instead, he grew more distracted.

Worry churned in her stomach every time he glanced elsewhere. Something had him agitated. The regular looks over his shoulders and hard stares into the trees made him seem anxious to get away from her and their little trip. No matter how many times she tried to pull him into conversation, he let silence wash back over them.

"And bingo was his name-o."

"Mhm," Alex answered.

Liv gave up. She stopped in her tracks and planted her hands on her hips. "Alex. You're not listening to me."

"I am, I promise."

"Then tell me what I just said."

The gears turned in his head and his eyebrows drew together in a rough scowl when he couldn't come up with anything.

"Fine," he growled. "Just a little preoccupied."

"With whatever happened last night?"

A pit grew in her stomach as silence dragged on between them. All the imagined reasons why he left her in the first place came tumbling back, fresh as ever. There was someone else. He was just stringing her along. He liked the chase more than the real thing.

Maybe they were pushing things too soon. Maybe she'd made a mistake getting close to him again.

Working to keep her voice steady, she squared up to him and put her cards on the table. "I need you to be in this, or I'm out. I'm not going down this path where I'm suddenly dropped all over again."

"It's not you," Alex sighed heavily. "It's me."

Liv threw her hands in the air. "You expect me to just trust that? The same could be said of last time."

"This isn't like last time. It's—" He cut himself off with a growl and shifted his look somewhere over her shoulder. He ran a hand down his face and met her eyes again. "I'm sorry, okay? There's just something heavy on my mind."

"Then let me in. I can't do anything but worry if you won't tell me what's wrong." She softened her tone and reached a hand out to him. Warmth spread up her arm as soon as her palm touched his arm. "I don't want a repeat of before. I want to know what has you looking over your shoulder every thirty seconds and avoiding the conversation."

"It's not—"

"I swear to all that's holy, I'll kick you in the balls right now if that sentence finishes with 'not your concern.'"

"I was going to say 'not something for you to worry about,' but have at it." Alex tossed her an infuriating smirk and gestured at his crotch.

Liv ground her teeth together, but didn't take the bait. "That's some mighty fine deflection there. And if that's how you want to play it, I'll just turn back around right now."

ALEX WATCHED Liv's face harden. Her expression shuttered and locked him out. Prickly anger scented the air and irritated his nose.

Fuck, he'd wanted to avoid that.

Dammit. She was right. He wasn't in his right mind. Hadn't been since the day before when he found her picture stuck to his door. His monster lurked somewhere and he couldn't even trust his own damn senses to pinpoint the danger. Bastard had a way of hiding himself until he wanted to be found. Too quick, too stealthy, he appeared and disappeared before anyone knew he was there.

And Liv wanted to know everything when he could hardly even think about the incident without wanting to shift and tear into the entire fucking world.

The basket bumped against his leg and he growled in irritation. Stupid fucking basket. He dropped it to the ground and paced, not even caring about the bottles that rattled inside. Bringing her anywhere out in the open had been an idiot idea in the first place.

Alex growled and shoved his hands in his hair. "Have you gotten any other threats at work?"

"What does that have to do—"

"Liv, just answer. Please."

"No. Nothing recently." She pressed her lips in a thin line. "Are you still going on about that? I told you, we all get them."

"Not like this, you don't." His bear shoved forward, ready to make the world run red. He swallowed hard and worked to form the words. "It came from my maker."

Liv raised a hand to her throat. The hardness in her eyes dropped immediately and shock entered her scent. "You're sure?" she asked softly. "But how—Why?"

"To fuck with me, I'm sure." His laugh sounded hollow to his own ears. Liv grimaced. "Maybe it was just a huge fucking coincidence and I led him right to you. But now? Liv, he pinned your picture to my front door with a damn knife!"

"Holy shit." Her face paled, and she stumbled back until she rested against a tree trunk. "You're sure? What am I saying, of course you're sure. You're the one with the nose."

Alex stepped closer and landed his hands on her hips. He twitched up the hem of her shirt and stroked his thumbs against her skin. Heat flared to life and spread through him, but he doused it quickly.

He couldn't keep her. It was selfish to think he could. She needed someone better. Someone with a future.

"I'm so sorry." He shut his eyes. He couldn't see plain blossom there again. "You should leave."

Liv dismissed the idea with a rude noise that snapped his eyes open. "Don't be stupid. I'm not going anywhere."

"It isn't safe for you here," he insisted. "I can't give you the life you deserve. I don't have a future. Not with him around."

"Okay, so we take precautions. The research facility is practically in lockdown. I'll be safe during work hours. We can get Sloan involved. Surely she has resources with the SEA."

She already had a thousand different possible solutions. He loved that her mind never stopped working.

Too bad they were ideas he'd discarded as not good enough. Hell, even sticking to her side all day, every day wasn't enough. For his bear, yes. The beast wanted nothing else. But for practicalities? Her safety? She needed to be locked inside a bunker deep in the mountains with the armies of ten nations surrounding her before he'd relax in the slightest.

She cupped his cheek. "Stop. I can see all those doubts running wild in your eyes."

"I'm dangerous, Liv."

"You shifted around me just fine."

"After almost biting you." His throat bobbed with a hard swallow. "The threats to me extend to you."

"Did you bring me out here to get me day drunk or break up with me?"

Alex blinked at the sudden switch of subject. "Implying we're dating?"

She threw him a crooked smile. "You can order me to leave or even abandon me in the middle of nowhere. I didn't come to Bearden for you, Alex. I'm sure as hell not leaving, either."

"You really know how to make a man feel wanted."

"I know my worth, is all." She leaned up and pressed her lips to his. "We have to be careful. Noted. I'm not leaving. So either bust out those mimosas or say the words. You're not getting off easy this time."

Alex huffed a laugh. Just like that, she'd inserted herself into his life. His bear still paced through his head and his shoulders were still as tense as rocks, but something loosened in his chest.

She was his.

Maybe Ethan was right. He could make this work and keep her safe.

He stiffened, nostrils flaring. A growl rattled in his throat even before he turned.

Not thirty feet from them, standing between two trees, was his maker.

"Bastard," Alex growled. His fists clenched at his sides as white-hot rage flooded his veins. His bear surged forward. Fur pricked his arms and claws tipped his fingernails. Sendings flowed from his inner beast, each of them crimson with the blood he needed to taste.

Years went into the response. The trauma of those first few shifts, the pain of leaving the woman once again at his side. All the fights and brawls and shifts needed to keep him as close to steady as possible.

That bastard caused it all.

Bright green eyes watched him with amusement before turning to Liv.

"Alex, who's that?" she asked with a trace of panic in her voice.

"Run," he ordered. His voice was thick with the shift already on him.

His muscles tensed. There was no putting his shift on pause, no fleeing the scene. His bear snarled at the threat in front of him. The threat to his mate. The bastard had already ruined one life; he wouldn't be allowed to get near Liv and ruin hers, too.

His bear ripped out of him, sending Liv scrambling backward.

Still, she didn't run.

Alex jumped for her and roared, intending to scare her into action. Liv gasped and jerked back, falling to the ground. Stinging fear overrode every tangy, tasty part of her scent.

Everything except the blood.

A line of it stretched from her hip to her knee. Red spread over her jeans from the fresh wound.

Alex whirled and roared. Not just at the bastard in front of him, but at himself. He caused her fear and pain. He didn't deserve her.

But he'd sure as hell fight until his dying breath for her.

He lunged for his bastard of a maker, rising up on hind legs to slam his paw into the bear's face. Another blow caught him in the shoulder, then he, too, was on his back legs and swinging. Overtures complete, they settled into the intricate dance of enemies wishing to spill lifeblood in the dirt.

Back and back. He drove the bastard away from his mate still bleeding and scared.

Monster, monster, monster.

Him or the bastard who changed him?

He roared with fury at not knowing.

He needed to be put down before he hurt her even worse.

Just as soon as he made sure he was the only threat to her alive.

Alex lunged again for his maker, fury driving his every blow.

CHAPTER 19

Liv sucked down breath after breath and willed her heart to stop racing. She could hardly hear over the rush in her ears and she needed to listen closely to the rustling crash of plant life around her. Somewhere, the two bears clashed. The grunts and roars of each were distinctly furious with the promise of violence.

Too close. They were still too close for her comfort. A mile would be too close. Five. Existing on the same planet with the other one, Alex's monster, made her skin crawl.

And he wanted her. She'd become a target for him in his pursuit of Alex. Her stomach twisted itself in knots trying to comprehend the grotesque drive to utterly destroy someone.

Liv looked around helplessly. Her leg ached. She pressed shaking fingers to the wound. Not too deep, luckily, but pain still blasted through her nerves. She grimaced as she forced herself to her feet. Her head spun, more because of the events than blood loss. She hoped.

What the fucking *fuck*.

Shock. She had to be in shock.

Alone in the woods with monsters all around. She couldn't stand still like bait. She had to move.

Her shaking was mostly under control by the time she limped off the trail and to the parking lot. She tried the door of Alex's truck before she remembered he'd stuffed his keys in his pocket when they first arrived. A pocket that was probably strewn about on the trail somewhere.

She cursed herself for not thinking about keys and chewed her lower lip. The parking lot was starting to fill—the reason why Alex wanted to go so early in the morning. She crossed her arms over the edge of the pickup bed to hide her leg and look like she simply waited on someone's arrival. She didn't want any questions or concerns while she put her thoughts in order.

Maybe he'd come back.

Did she want that?

Each blink, and the scene played out on the back of her eyelids. Her own mini movie screen and she couldn't control the picture.

Alex roaring. At her. At the other bear.

His jaws snapping shut. His breath rushed out in a hot blast with his snarl.

Oh, the noises. Those were as real to her as if she were back on the ground all over again. The savage sound rattling out of both bears. The slapping of huge paws against one another as they battled, one trying to push toward her and the other driving that bastard away. The crashing, thudding, banging, growling, snarling, vicious noises of a war between beasts.

No. At that moment, all she wanted was to be back in her bed with her covers over her head and no one around to hear her cry it out.

Liv reached in her pocket and pulled out her phone, thankful it hadn't fallen out or been crushed when she hit the ground.

When Alex shoved her down.

Liv blinked back the rush of messy, complicated emotions and dialed Sloan's number. She must have sounded shakier than she thought because Sloan agreed to pick her up right away, no questions asked.

Still, she couldn't help but glance over her

shoulder every ten seconds. Her pulse spiked whenever a puff of air rustled the leaves, but the noise never turned out to be Alex or the other bear.

Liv would have been dancing with anxiety if she could move easily by the time Sloan turned into the parking lot.

The other woman's mouth fell open as soon as Liv turned toward her Jeep. She jumped out of her seat and immediately grabbed an elbow to help Liv hobble to the other side. "What the fuck happened?"

"'Tis but a scratch," Liv muttered.

Sloan dropped her eyes to her thigh, then raised them back to Liv's face. "Flesh wound or not, that's some damage. Care to clue me in?"

Liv slumped down in her seat. Tears welled in her eyes and her hands shook again. "Alex," she muttered. "Alex shoved me down."

"Alex did this?" Sloan's voice turned murderous and her hands tightened on the door.

"He was protecting me. I think."

"Okay, protecting you or not, you need to get to a doctor." Sloan rounded the hood and climbed back into the driver's seat.

Liv shook her head the whole time. "I just want to go home. Please, Sloan. Just take me home."

Sloan took a hard look at her thigh again. Her jaw tightened as she weighed the pros and cons. "If you're sure," she finally said, hesitation heavy in her voice. "But I'm calling the rest of the clan. They need to know what happened." She typed out a quick message on her phone and fixed Liv with a serious look. "Which means you need to tell me everything."

Liv stared straight ahead and nodded. She drew a shaky breath and tried to figure out a starting point while Sloan twisted the key of her Jeep and started out of the parking lot. That morning? Or from the unmarked letter she'd received at work. No, Sloan already knew that happened, except not in relation to everything else.

"It was the one that bit him," Liv said in a near whisper. "He's here. Alex said he's after me. He just... flipped out as soon as the other one got close. Told me to run. I don't know why I didn't. I wanted to help, but what could I have done against all that?" Liv covered her mouth with her hand and bit back the shrill note of laughter that bubbled out of her.

"Wanting to help someone else is a powerful response," Sloan agreed without judgment.

She'd never wished more for another side of herself. She wanted to be big and strong and powerful enough to blot out the hurt and fury in someone else. Alex needed help and she couldn't give it to him when it mattered the most.

"He just... was in my face. Roared. When I didn't move, he jumped for me and I fell backward. We got tangled up, I guess, and his claw caught me on the way down. Then he bounded toward the other bear. I've never seen such a vicious fight."

"Was that your first time up close to a shifter fight?" When she nodded, Sloan sighed. "They're rough, especially for us normies. Even seeing videos doesn't really prepare you for it."

"No. They really don't." Liv leaned her head against the window and stared at the passing trees.

Sloan didn't push for anything else and Liv was thankful for the silence. Something... wicked and ugly built in her chest. She didn't know whether she wanted to scream or cry. There was something brutally unfair about having a former relationship dropped back in her lap, letting herself think for even a moment all those unresolved issues finally had a happy ending, then seeing the curtain pulled aside to reveal something even more monstrous.

She was glad when Sloan turned into the little neighborhood for the research facility workers. Liv pushed open her door almost before Sloan pulled to a stop. She shot a miserable smile to her driver. "Thanks for the ride."

Sloan unbuckled her seatbelt and followed her out. "You're not getting rid of me that easily. Let me help you get cleaned up."

"I'm not a baby. I can do this on my own."

"Never said you were. You've seen a side of your man you haven't before and got a gnarly cut to show for it. You might be able to do this on your own, but you're not in a good spot."

Her man. Liv frowned. She didn't think those words were right anymore. Hadn't been for a long, long time. She'd been an idiot to think otherwise.

Yeah, she was in full pity party mode. Anyone objecting could see themselves out the door.

"Fine," she agreed.

Sloan jumped right into caregiver mode and ordered Liv out of her jeans and into the bathroom. Liv's grumble about needing dinner first was met with a steely look and a promise to cuff her and haul her to Bearden's clinic if she didn't cooperate.

Liv was soon seated on the edge of her tub with the first aid kit open at her side.

"I've gotten pretty good at this," Sloan mused. She

dug through the contents and pulled aside what she needed. "Between the other agents wanting to prove themselves through a good fight instead of working their damn caseload, and the madness on the ranch, I could probably be a certified nurse by now. This is going to sting a little."

"Do they fight often?" Liv asked.

Sloan made a face. "It's a good day when Alex is in only one brawl."

Once Sloan finished dressing her leg with enough bandages to wrap a mummy, in Liv's humble opinion, she said, "I'm going to update the others, then I'll be right back to check on you."

Liv gripped her wrist before she could leave the bathroom. "Promise me you won't do anything to him."

"He hurt you. Even if he didn't mean to, this still happened." Sloan shook her head, blue eyes hardening. "If he'd bitten you…"

He'd be no better than the one who hurt him in the first place. The same consequences would apply.

Death.

"He isn't too far gone. You have to believe me." Liv swallowed back the anguish she felt deep in her soul. "You want to help? Find the one who did this to him. He's the real monster."

Alex had tried to warn her. He'd given her every chance to turn away. She'd still pushed and prodded and wiggled her way closer. Some stupid part of her refused to understand he was different from the man she used to love.

He and his bear were one and the same, he said. Only, someone put that bear inside him and filled him with fury.

Alex scared her. Past the shock and anger for his situation and everything else, a mound of fear grew higher and higher. He'd protected her, yes. But his eyes had gone dead and animalistic. He'd clawed her up and snapped his jaws inches from her face.

He'd been right all along. She needed to stay away. Hell, maybe her entire family was right that supes were dangerous. If a vampire didn't want to suck her dry or a fae magic her to death, there was always the threat of claws and fangs from a shifter. Liv could already hear her mother demanding she return home and find a nice, unassuming husband and live out a quiet life.

"Sloan, please. I know what happens to out of control shifters. I know what the SEA does to them if their alphas won't step up and put them down." She had a way out if she wanted to take it. He didn't. She couldn't live with herself if Alex suffered. "That monster made him this way. Don't hurt him more."

The woman's expression shuttered. "That's going to be up to Ethan."

"Then tell me what I need to do to keep Alex alive."

CHAPTER 20

Alex was hunter and hunted. The target at his front put a target on his back. Too many were after him to outrun them for long. He just wanted to hold off the inevitable until he put down the bastard that threatened Liv.

Then he could let Ethan do what an alpha dreaded and put him down, too. He deserved it. He'd harmed a human.

Not just any human, either. His mate.

He'd snapped his jaws in her face and clawed up her leg. Either could have turned to fatal wounds. Sheer luck kept her from bleeding out at his feet.

He had one task to do, then he'd walk willingly to his funeral pyre.

His bear growled. At him, at the fate he chose,

Alex didn't care. They were one on the mission, their minds melding closer than ever before. At that moment, his maker's death was all that mattered. They could fight over the rest later.

It'd been two sunsets and a sunrise since he last walked on two feet. His maker led him up and down the mountains, in and out of the enclave, over rolling hills. Whenever Alex lost the scent, he returned to Liv's cabin. Her scent was cold and faint, but his maker's was fresh and strong.

Returning had been the trouble. He'd picked up a tail after the sunrise. More followed him as the day wore on and night fell. They stayed at a distance, never coming closer than a quarter mile. But they stuck to him no matter how he tried to throw them off the trail.

Still, he hunted. The ones at his back weren't his concern. He only wanted the bastard somewhere at his front.

Impossible, when the scent faded into nothing more often than not. His maker was an apparition.

Just like the visits at the ranch, the trail ended suddenly. He thought maybe the bear shifted and rode away in some vehicle, but the tread marks he found were too regularly used to pick out any one set.

So he retraced his steps and went back to square one, but no amount of sniffing brought new clues. The bastard was too clever to be caught.

Alex started to believe his maker was all in his head. He conjured up the spirit whenever he needed an excuse to focus his upset elsewhere. The monster of his past was the greatest scapegoat for his own slip into hellish behavior.

He needed a monstrous bastard to explain away harming his mate.

But no. The aches and pains up and down his body came from somewhere. Some brawling bear scored him with claws and fangs. He couldn't just imagine that. Could he?

Alex lifted a lip and snarled into the darkness. No. The sickly foul scent clogging his nose was too real. Too intrusive. It had branded itself on his brain the moment he first felt fangs tearing into his arms and legs.

He intended to return the favor. Questioning his sanity was just another torturous trick.

He paused at the crest of a hill. Moonlight glinted off the water below. Nothing moved, but he knew better than to trust his sight. He could taste his maker on each breath he drew. He was out there.

Somewhere. Faint scent or no scent at all, he was still alive and needed to be found.

Alex silently glided down the hill toward the stream. Bubbling water was a constant, dim, almost comforting sound. Somewhere in the distance, an owl hooted and dove a black shadow over the stream.

The place wasn't the same one he'd intended to sit with Liv beside while they ate and drank their fill, but the banks were similar enough that his heart ached to see her again. He wanted a lifetime of her laughs and only had his memories.

Giving in to the strong pull he felt for her had been a mistake. He'd been weak to let her sweet temptation lead him back to her bed. His maker saw it all and struck right where he'd hurt the most. Losing her all over again would destroy him.

Alex steeled himself. He'd lost her already. He'd make sure he brought another down with him. Then pyres and blissful death.

Movement rustled at the tree line. He bristled and whirled at the noise, ready to strike. A shadowy shape emerged, followed by two more. Each one smelled more of baked earth than forest and insanity.

Three lions ghosted along the stream, all eyes on

him. He growled and turned to go, only to be met by a bear at his back.

His growl rattled louder in his throat, but bright eyes simply watched him. He spun again and again, trying to keep the faint scent of his maker in his nose. He didn't have time for anyone else. Whatever they wanted could wait until he took down his prey.

More numbers joined them, until they were three lions and three bears, all with the single focus of drawing together tighter and tighter until he was stuck. He recognized the scents. Ashford clan and Crowley pride. They'd set aside their differences to hunt him down.

Alex roared with vicious violence and tried to push his way through the blockade. Lions and bears crowded around him and snapped him back into place.

Assholes! Couldn't they smell anything? They were letting his maker get away!

Maybe he was crazy after all.

Crazy enough to snap back and sink his claws anywhere he could reach. Desperation powered his blows. He needed to get free!

Grunts and growls met his ears, but they spiraled tighter and tighter, leaving him no space to move and barely any to breathe.

A rumble sounded in the distance, then lights slashed over the scene. Alex twisted in the tight confines of other bodies as a pickup truck bumped over the rough terrain. The lions called out, chuffing where the bears stayed silent.

Two men hopped out and walked to the edges of the shifting sea of fur. One ran his hands through his hair while the other simply cocked his head and bared his teeth. Alex let their scents rolled over him. Both were full of fur and dominance that made him snarl. Ethan's held worry, but Trent's was tinged with a hint of the fury and madness that drove Alex on.

Trent lifted a rifle to his shoulder.

Not yet, Alex pleaded. He wasn't ready yet. He still had blood to draw.

"It's time to come home," Ethan said. "You're going to hurt someone out here."

Already had. The scent of Liv's fear haunted him.

He snarled and whipped his head from side to side. Running and hunting were better on four feet. He didn't need to see her pain again. He didn't have to face the shame of harming his mate.

"Liv has been asking for you."

Alex's heart seized.

"She's staying at the ranch. We've watched over

her for you. Kept her safe," Ethan continued. "I don't know what to tell her."

Nothing. His human side wanted to spit. He had no words to offer her. No tenderness to make things right. He'd hurt her. He'd done it before and he did it again and he'd just keep doing it if he stayed close to her. He was fucked in the head. He couldn't keep a mate. Couldn't cherish her the way she needed. One misstep, and he drew her blood.

He needed to pay for that sin.

His bear, though, paused.

She was their mate. She needed them.

"Shift," his alpha ordered.

He shook off the command. He didn't want to obey. Couldn't. Not when his monster still walked the earth.

"Alex, last warning. Shift and make this easy on everyone."

Fuck that.

He slammed through the bodies blocking him and pawed at the earth. Red swam in his vision. He wouldn't be ordered around.

He charged.

"Take him," Ethan ordered.

A sharp noise, then a sting in his shoulder.

Alex stumbled forward as the tranquilizer blasted

through his system. His front legs crumpled underneath him. His spine tingled, then numbed as the world darkened down to twin pinpoints of light.

Then those, too, were gone.

When he woke again, he was in a cage.

CHAPTER 21

T he rest of Saturday passed without a word or sign from Alex.

Word of what happened spread like wildfire within the clan. The ranch was full of activity from the moment Liv pulled to a stop in front of the main house with Sloan right behind her. Tansey settled her into a room upstairs and the waiting began.

Sunday, one of the others spotted Alex. Ethan headed up the mission to track him down, but there'd been no update by the time Tansey convinced her to trudge up to bed and try to find some sleep.

Liv felt like shit on Monday morning. Her heart pounded much too fast. She felt achy and flushed even though her temperature was normal. Her stomach revolted against the idea of joining the others downstairs for breakfast. Dark bags lined her eyes from all the sleep she'd abandoned after an hour or two of staring at the ceiling above her bed.

She missed Alex. Worry for him ran almost as strong, but the hole in her heart and the pit in her stomach throbbed constantly. She felt like she'd lost him all over again. Alone in her apartment or alone in the woods, the same sharp sorrow filled her as before.

The noises downstairs faded to nothing by the time she found the will to roll out of bed. She washed her face and dressed for the day, then steeled herself enough to walk down the stairs.

The house was unusually quiet. The few days she'd been there always had something going on. Tansey and Joss never seemed far from the kitchen. The men wandered in and out between their other tasks. Even Sloan was a frequent face when not on duty.

Truthfully, the quiet was both unnerving and welcome. Liv didn't want more looks of pity or quiet words meant to make her feel better. She wanted Alex.

Liv paused at the great fireplace and studied the pictures lining the mantle. Some were old, with faces she didn't recognize. Newer ones dotted the collection, most with the happy couples she knew. Despite the attempted scowls on the men's faces, she could still see the obvious affection in their eyes.

One of Ethan snagged her attention. She picked it up for a closer look. He had his arm wrapped around a younger woman with features similar to his own and lighter hair. A relation, Liv guessed, since Tansey, Joss, and Sloan were the only mates on the ranch. They hadn't mentioned anyone else during the movie night, either.

"My sister."

Liv startled at Ethan's voice. She glanced over her shoulder and found him right behind her. He reached around her and plucked the picture from her hands. "Where is she?"

"Third year of university in Bozeman." A ghost of a smile passed over Ethan's face as he settled the frame back into place. "I wish she'd find a man and stay there."

Liv scoffed. "You sound just like my mother. She nearly had a stroke when I told her I wanted to go to grad school."

"Not like that. Colette has ideas of coming back here and nursing our sick animals and turning the ranch around. She could do anything she wanted. No reason for her to be tied down to this place."

"And you think if she finds someone, they'll keep her away."

"I know finding your mate is the best thing in the world. I want her to have that happiness and know someone has her back through the good and the bad." His second smile was bigger and lasted for more than a second. "And maybe I won't need my kid sister in my business every damn day."

"You really care for her."

"I care for them all." His eyes flicked to the next picture over. The men of the Black Claw clan hung out the windows or perched on the hood of a truck covered in mud. "But sometimes caring isn't enough."

Her heart jumped to her throat. "Did you find him?"

Instead of answering, he turned toward the kitchen. He went right for the cabinet with the booze and pulled out a bottle of whiskey and two glasses. "This isn't an easy life," he said as he poured amber liquid into both.

Liv drew in a deep breath and released it slowly as she approached. Drinking came naturally to the wild clan, but so early? Shaky nerves and bad news went with a stiff drink before noon.

"We're a little wilder out here. Prone to brawling and broken bones. My bears all have inner demons and struggle to keep steady. I've tried to give them all a place to get their heads on right and carve out a life for themselves." Ethan slid her a glass and took a swig from his own, mouth set in a grim line.

"Did you find him?" Liv repeated.

A muscle jumped in his jaw. He stared hard into his glass and took another swallow. "A good alpha takes up the role hoping they will help their people. Sometimes they aren't enough. Sometimes the demons win."

Liv ignored the room swimming around her and planted her hands on the table. She didn't like the direction of the conversation. She liked Ethan's coddling even less. "Did you," she started in a hard voice, "find him?"

"We need to take a drive." Ethan slammed back the rest of his drink and stood, then nodded at hers. "Drink up. I need you steady and brave."

Heart still lodged in her throat, Liv gulped down her drink under Ethan's watchful eye. As soon as she was done, he strode for the door.

Liv didn't know what to expect or where she'd be

taken. She clung to the one hope that had kept her going as the days faded into nights and brought sunrises filled with new worry.

Alex had to be alive.

In bad condition, sure, but still alive. Ethan would have said something otherwise instead of preparing her with a drink and taking her elsewhere.

Instead of turning toward town, Ethan swung the other direction and turned into the next ranch.

Signs warned visitors away with rude curses. Ethan ignored them all and bumped along the single track road, not unlike the one leading to the heart of Black Claw Ranch.

But they didn't pass any buildings. At some point, Ethan turned off the road and onto a faint path. They crested hills and drove through a herd of cattle, all while Liv's nerves sparked together and didn't give her a moment of peace. So much for the drink.

Ethan cursed as he pulled to a stop in front of a small hill with a dark opening at its base. One other truck sat nearby. "This is going to be hard. Let me do the talking, okay?"

"What? Why?"

"Because Trent hates humans, and he's the one standing guard right now."

Liv turned her head slowly. "Why does he need to stand guard?"

"You'll see soon enough."

As soon as the truck shut off, another man stepped out of the dark opening. He didn't raise a hand in greeting or change his stony expression. When Liv pushed out of her door, his nostrils flared. "You brought a human on my land?"

Ethan shrugged. "She needs to see this."

"On my land," the man repeated in a growl. "Fucking humans don't understand shit, and you brought one on my land."

"It's her right."

Trent spat on the ground and pointed at her. "Not my fault if her guts get spilled on the ground."

Liv opened her mouth and snapped it back closed with a glare from Ethan. Irritation pooled in her middle at both men, but Trent in particular. Abrasive was the kindest word she could think of to describe him.

"She won't do anything stupid," Ethan promised.

Trent's rebuttal sounded in the back of his throat, but he canted his head to the side and stomped into the darkness.

Liv glanced at Ethan. He grimaced and dipped his chin, but followed. She was left with staying out in the sun and in safety or stepping into the darkness to find some answers.

A roar sounded from inside the cave.

Liv chose darkness.

Her eyes adjusted to the low light. The cave wasn't large. The roof wasn't much taller than Ethan or Trent's heads. Two of her with arms stretched wide could hold hands and touch the walls. She didn't know much about caves, but she was certain the place wasn't naturally made.

One of the men in front of her bent to fiddle with something at his feet. A lantern sparked to life as he straightened and Liv gasped.

Ethan and Trent nearly blocked the view, but their shoulders couldn't mute the growls echoing around the small chamber.

Liv pushed between them. A giant, black bear paced behind thick, silver bars. Every couple of steps, he swiped at the bars or tried to bite them. Bright green eyes jumped from face to face and she knew who was locked inside.

"You put him in a cage?" She rounded on Ethan and Trent. "Why?"

"You'd rather have him roaming and fighting anything that moves?" Trent snapped.

"This is how it ends when we lose control of our beasts," Ethan said in a gentler voice.

Liv shook her head, her blood running cold. She knew what he meant. Sloan had implied it as well. Hell, even Alex predicted his future was a short one.

Sometimes the demons won.

"No," Liv denied fiercely. She wouldn't lose him again. "That's not happening. He's not too far gone. I refuse to let you put him down like a rabid animal."

"Ain't no cure when they start foaming at the mouth," Trent muttered. He rolled his eyes to Ethan. "Thought you said she was smart."

Her shock at seeing Alex caged boiled into a rage. He'd been turned against his will and harassed over the years. He'd lost friends and family and uprooted his entire life. When a glimmer of hope and happiness came along, that bastard that hurt him came back to burn it all to the ground again.

And the people he called his clan wanted to kill him.

Not on her life.

Liv marched the few steps between them and shoved a finger under Trent's nose. "Fuck you. That's a person in there."

Trent wrapped his fingers around her wrist and

squeezed tight. The bear roared and banged against the bars of the cage. "There's nothing in there. Look for yourself," he growled, eyes flashing pure amber. He twisted her around and shoved her closer to the cage. "The human side of him was just another meal for his animal. Putting him down would be a damn mercy."

Liv steadied herself. The bear dropped back to all fours. His roar died down to a constant growl. He paced the few steps back and forth he could manage, never taking his bright green eyes off her.

They looked even wilder than when she last saw him.

"I can't believe that," she said without turning. Fuck Trent. She wouldn't let him see the tears welling in her eyes. "He's in there somewhere. I won't let you kill him."

"Listen, little girl—"

"Trent," Ethan snapped. "A day more costs us nothing."

There was a pause, but Liv still didn't look behind her. She put her entire focus on Alex, if she could even call him that. As much as she didn't want to hear the words, Trent was right. There was no intelligence in the eyes that watched her. The growls and huffed breaths were that of an animal trying to figure out how to get to his prey. She wasn't Liv to him; she was just another meal.

"Fine," Trent said finally. "Not my problem when he chews her to bits. I'm not the one putting him down."

Hard footsteps stomped away, then softer ones approached her. "What happened?" she asked.

"We found him roaming about fifty miles from here. Probably still hunting for the one that attacked you. He wouldn't listen to an alpha order to shift back, so we drugged him and brought him here. He wasn't even conscious again when the bear took back over and shifted him while he slept. He refuses to shift and attacks anyone that gets near."

"There's nothing you can do?"

"I've tried everything in my power. He's grown unsteady over the years. Fighting more, both in fur and skin. He's gotten close to refusing orders, but always backed down. You coming into town made him a little better. This time is different. He feels…" Ethan grimaced and rubbed a hand over his heart, "broken."

Liv squeezed her eyes shut. A tear rolled down her cheek. She pressed her lips together and held back the wave of anguish that threatened to shake her shoulders with sobs.

"I don't want him to die," Ethan said softly. "I also don't want him to be a danger to anyone else."

"Then let me try."

"You have the day." He reached for a shoulder and turned her. "If anyone can reach him, it'll be his mate."

Mate? Hah. Not likely, with the man she wanted locked away inside some mad beast. If he even existed.

No. She couldn't let that belief creep up on her. She had to hold out hope that they were handed a second chance for a reason. Improbable, unlikely, unscientific, she didn't care. Hope for a fate that didn't involve mourning Alex was all she had left.

Liv turned back to the cage and nodded. After a moment, Ethan followed Trent out of the cave and left her alone with the bear.

"Okay," Liv breathed. "Okay. We can fix this. Can't we?"

The bear raised a lip and snarled.

"You know, there are easier ways to dump a girl than going beast mode and losing your humanity." Liv took a seat on the cold stone. She traced the subtle bumps and cracks of the cave floor. They grounded her in the moment. "In fact, I'm not letting you off the hook this time. You got away without answers years ago. If you want me gone, you've got to use your words and tell me."

The bear rushed the bars and slammed into them. Liv jumped and eyed where they were sunk into the ground and ceiling. All the connections appeared solid, as did the bars themselves.

Liv drew in a big breath and spoke over the growls.

"Remember that time when we went to the Fourth of July party at Hank's Fun-n-Buns? There was a costume contest and everything. You went as Sexy Uncle Sam. Red and white striped hot pants that I swore were so tight you'd be showing off your bits by the second hour. We spent an entire afternoon trying to find the perfect blue blazer to go with it, only for some drunk freshman to run into you with a plate of wings."

Liv huffed a laugh at the memory of dull orange sauce drying on the cloth. There'd been no saving the jacket or the costume. Alex had quickly gone from Sexy Uncle Sam to a shirtless guy in hot pants. A fair number of women eyed him up, but she'd been the one to peel him out of those damn shorts at the end of the night.

"That was right after we moved in together. Do you remember that old hag that tried to block us from using the freight elevator? She insisted she'd been waiting since dawn and we had to let her go first. Then it turned out she had her delivery date wrong and screamed at whatever poor soul picked up the phone at the furniture store. I thought the property manager was going to call the cops on her."

The bear sat back. His growl stopped and she plowed on with renewed determination. She didn't care if it was simply the sound of a soothing voice instead of the harsh voices of Trent and Ethan. Something had his attention.

She jumped from memory to memory. Good ones and bad ones. She even resolved old arguments and taunted him with her one-sided victories. There was simply nothing like gaining the agreement of a bear over how to load the dishwasher or stack the cookie sheets and pans.

Eventually, though, her rush of memories sputtered to a stop. She didn't know which ones helped, if they did at all. The bear watched her and paced in turn, never seeming to understand her words.

Liv sighed and drew her legs to her chest. "I don't know what I'm doing," she admitted. "I was so lost after you left. Hurt and angry, yeah, but lost. Even when everyone told me it was time to move on, I found excuses. I needed to work on myself or I was too busy with applying for lab positions. I hated whenever someone tried to set me up because I knew they'd never compare to you."

Too many first, last dates. Pushy kissers. Pushy friends. Frustration over where she stood and where she wanted to be. She'd filled those years with work and overtime because that was easier to accept than a silent apartment.

All because she missed Alex.

"My mom would love for me to go home and find a boring husband to settle down with. So you'd better quit it with this bullshit and change back because that's not the life I want." Liv laid her cheek on her knees. "I want you, Alex."

He'd scared her. Shocked her. Hell, even hurt her. She could deal with all that if it got her what she wanted: a wild man who made her laugh and love life.

She hated everything he'd gone through and wished things could have been different. If they'd happened just a few years later, maybe he wouldn't have needed to run. Maybe they'd have moved to Bearden and started their lives instead of taking the shitty long way around.

But wishes weren't reality, and she had a broken bear sitting in front of her.

Fuck the bastard that hurt him. She wouldn't let him win. Alex was hers. She'd stick by his side. He deserved the loyalty.

"You're better with me. That's what Ethan said. That's what I believe." She edged closer to the cage and looked right into the bright green eyes. Nothing more than animal sparked in them, but she kept going. She had the day. She'd use every damn minute. "You hurt me, Alex, but you have to believe you're nothing like the monster that turned you. What you did was an accident. What he did was a fucked up crime. You're better than him. Believe that down to your bones. You're flawed, imperfect, and complicated. But you are good. You are mine."

Something flickered in his eyes.

"Mine, Alex," she whispered. She held her breath, heart fluttering with hope.

The bear shook his head and pawed at his nose.

Then there was a loud *snap* followed by a roar.

The bear's shape shimmered and popped. Fur melted back and Liv gasped. Tears sprang to her eyes as the beast slowly ceded to the man.

"Alex!"

Seconds passed into a minute, then another. Alex panted and stared at the ceiling, then he rolled her face toward her.

"Where's the key?" he asked in a rough rasp.

Liv laughed and scrubbed at her cheeks. "I don't know."

"What kind of person agrees to babysit someone in a cave and doesn't get the key?" Alex grinned through his grumble. "Come here. Even if you can't let me out, I can still touch you."

Liv crawled forward until she could reach through the bars. Alex reached, too, though how he didn't pinch his big arms was beyond her.

Then he wrapped her close and Liv didn't even care they were smooshed together with silver bars between them.

She had him and she wouldn't give him up again.

CHAPTER 22

The sound of the shower running brought Alex out of sleep. He threw a hand wide, already knowing he'd find the bed cold and empty. Unless someone had broken into his home, Liv was the one using up all the hot water. Just like she'd done most mornings since she shoved him back from the edge.

A growl vibrated in his chest, pleased once again. She'd done the impossible.

He hadn't been able to let her go after that. And thankfully, she'd put up with his shit. Moving her into his home was one demand. Seeing her constantly guarded was another. His maker was still on the loose and still terrorized his dreams, but little by little, Alex breathed easier knowing Liv fell asleep in his den and stole his hot water the next morning.

They'd slipped so easily into old habits and made new ones as one week turned into two. Dinners and breakfasts and stolen moments knotted them closer and closer together.

There was just one looming crack in their happiness. One fucking prick that kept him awake at nights and made his vision swim with red. One asshole kept the days from utter perfection.

Alex rumbled a growl and rolled out of bed. Fuck those thoughts. Perfection waited on the other side of the cracked bathroom door.

He slipped inside and shut the door with a click to give Liv warning of his arrival.

Alex drew open the curtain and let his eyes feast on the delicious sight in front of him. He knew every dip and swell of Liv's gorgeous body. He'd mapped the inches with his fingers and tongue. He didn't think he'd ever get enough.

And with a heaping dish of luck he didn't deserve, maybe he wouldn't have to.

Blood rushed straight to his cock and he couldn't stop a quick pump as he stepped in and closed the curtain behind him.

"You got up early," he murmured into the crooked of her neck. Her skin against his calmed the itching between his shoulders. Selfish, maybe, but he leaned on her when his bear couldn't shake loose of thoughts of his maker. She kept him steady.

Liv wiped the water from her eyes and turned into him. She wrapped her arms around him and pulled him close. "It's this new thing I'm trying."

"Hm?" Tangy, sweet scent filled his nose. Responsive, sensitive woman. Ready for him within seconds. His hands skimmed up her sides and cupped her breasts. He sought the hard peaks of her nipples, rolling them between his fingers.

Liv arched into his touch and her teeth caught her lower lip with her soft sigh. "It's called not being late."

Alex leaned over her. His lips ghosted against hers "Where's the fun in that?"

"Oh," she laughed in a throaty chuckle. She wrapped a hand around his cock and worked him with firm, hard strokes. "There's still plenty of fun."

Liv wiggled out of his grasp and slid down to her knees. She pumped his shaft again, then drew her tongue from his balls to his tip and swirled around his head.

Water splashed all around him. Alex shoved his hair back to clear the strands from his eyes. He didn't want to miss a single thing.

"Tease," he admonished.

Liv rolled her eyes upward. The stormy grey color simmered with need. The look alone almost had him close to release.

She sucked him deep, cheeks hollowing, and forced another groan from him. Her tongue curled around him, stroking as she slid up and down. Her mouth worked magic.

Those lusty eyes watched him as she slid a hand down her body and touched herself. Small moans mixed with his and the scent of her arousal exploded in the air.

"Fuck," he groaned.

Alex lost the battle for control and fisted his hand into Liv's hair. Her tongue flattened, and he thrust between her lips.

Waves of heat billowed around him. Water and steam from the shower. An inferno of lust ignited by the woman on her knees. He was cloaked in a fire that licked down his spine and drew his balls tight.

"Liv," he groaned. Or growled. Was it even her name he pushed between his lips? Or some plea to the heavens for strength and release?

He needed to be inside her. Needed to feel her come around him before he let himself go.

He tugged her away from him and urged her to her feet. Alex slid his hands around to her ass and she jumped, trusting him to catch her. His heart threatened to pound its way out of his chest.

"*Alex.*"

Liv nipped at his neck and crashed him back to the very sweet, very sexy reality of a woman with her legs wrapped around his waist and spread open for him. Liquid heat coated him as he rocked his hips against her and drew a throaty groan from her.

He thrust inside, cock pressing deep. Her body clamped down and squeezed him tight. So tight. So fucking, amazingly tight.

Heaven existed right between her legs.

Silky muscles fluttered around him. He eased back with slow deliberation. Tease, he'd called her, but the choked noises in her throat flung the accusation back in his face.

Alex grinned against her lips. He breathed her in, consumed every sound that spilled from her chest. She gasped when he filled her to the brim and moaned when he pulled back. Hard and slow, rough and gentle.

"More," she moaned.

A growl rattled in his throat. Sendings punched at him and made his gums ache.

Bite. Mark. Claim.

He wanted everything she had to offer. Her body. Her mind. Her everlasting love. All of it was his for the taking.

"Mine," he growled.

He thrust harder. Faster. Her body molded to the rhythm he set. He dragged gasps and moans from her and met them with grunts and growls of his own.

"And you're mine." Grey eyes watched him, shining as bright as any shifter's. There wasn't an animal under her skin—he'd made sure of that, even if he'd hurt her in the process. No, something greater watched him. Something huge and important and too big for words at that precise moment.

Alex nodded, the only response he could spare. He didn't know how to do any of this.

She was his mate, that was clear as day. But she hadn't entirely burned out the darkness inside him.

That beast under his skin could still hurt her. Still wanted to make the world bleed if he couldn't get claws in the bastard that fucked up his life to begin with.

She trusted him, but he didn't trust himself.

"Alex!"

Pant, plea, he only heard the need in her voice.

His mate needed him.

Alex sealed his lips to hers and fucked into her harder, trying to wash away the doubts. If the world had any mercy left for him, they'd circle the drain and flow far, far away.

Liv was everything. He couldn't give her up.

And he couldn't complete their bond.

Not until his demons were finally put to rest.

Ripples danced along his length. She was close. He wanted her pleasure.

Her nails bit into his arms, his shoulders, his scalp. He bore each temporary mark with pride. They were all he could wear at that moment.

Alex bucked into her, again and again. A familiar tingle settled in the base of his spine. He slid deeper, harder, and Liv exploded all around him.

His hips jerked, shortening to shallow thrusts, drawing out her release as long as he could before he slammed into her to find his own pleasure. Alex snarled against her neck as her fingers drove into his hair. Warmth flooded out of him in a wave of heat.

She was light. Pure, perfect light. In that moment,

held by her and feeling her all around him, he could forget that monsters still existed in the world. His heart swelled simply being near her. Holding her was almost better than sex itself.

Almost.

Alex held her pressed against the tile and slowly sipped at her lips until the water started to cool, unable to let her go.

"We're going to be late," she murmured against his lips and wiggled.

Fuck. Alex squeezed his eyes closed on a groan. She felt too damn good. His cock twitched inside her.

He pressed his lips to hers, intending only for a final soft kiss. But then that wasn't enough. He growled low and swept his tongue against the seam of her lips until she parted for him. She met him stroke for stroke, tangling her fingers in his hair and clinging tightly to him.

"Don't want to go anywhere," he rasped in a rough voice when he eased back.

"That sounds like an easy way for you to get bored of me."

He cupped her cheeks and grazed his thumbs against her soft skin. Soft and unmarred. That was important. He hadn't hurt her in the weeks since she stood in front of an oncoming train and demanded it halt. She'd brought him back from the brink of certain death.

He hadn't claimed her, either.

His bear lodged a rumbled complaint that Alex dismissed.

"I will *never* get bored of you," he promised harshly.

Doubt flickered in her scent and across her face. "Good." She nipped his lower lip and ducked her eyes. "But you'll definitely need to invest in a bigger water heater. And learn to love pruned skin. Really, maybe rethink the whole keeping of us in the shower. There's a whole world out there to explore."

His bear paced through his head at her ramble. He let her slide to her feet, but didn't step away. He couldn't. Not with unease prickling his skin. "What's really on your mind?"

"You were out late again," she said gently. "And when you did sleep, you tossed and turned all night."

Fuck. *Fuck.* The pieces of his world sifted through his hands. No matter how hard he tried, he couldn't keep himself steady. Unfinished business kept him on the prowl and threatened the brief happiness he found with Liv.

"Hey." Liv pressed her hands to his cheeks. "Hey.

Quiet that growl there, bad bear. You're here with me. We're safe. There's nothing to worry about."

"Sorry," he said gruffly and wrenched out of her grasp. He rinsed quickly and stepped out, giving her space to finish up her shower.

Alex scrubbed a towel over his hair and wrapped it around his waist. A swipe across the mirror cleared enough fog for him to see himself—wild, glowing eyes and a chest that rose and fell too quickly.

Liv followed him a second later, wrapping herself in the towel hanging from a hook she'd claimed as her own. Worry drew her brows together. Most people would see him on the brink of a shift and run in the other direction. Not her. Brave woman wouldn't leave his side even when all signs pointed to the end of the line.

He planted his hands on the counter and flexed his fingers. In the mirror, he met her gaze. Soft. Too soft for his world. Too good. He hated that his maker had tried to hurt her. Hated that he'd been the one to actually put claws against her skin.

"We're not safe." Agitation spiked his heart rate as he gave voice to the darkness still inside him. "Not really. How long until he tries again? What if I'm not there next time?"

He closed his eyes and saw the blood on her leg. On her throat. Skies above, she'd tamed his inner beast, but monsters still lurked in the dark.

That was why he roamed at night. Those thoughts kept him up late. Every time he let himself relax even an inch, they crept up on him in stark reminder of what he could lose.

His mate.

His bear roared a challenge at the world. No one would take her. No one would touch her. Not while they still drew breath.

Liv crossed the small space. Her arms wrapped around his chest and her cheek pressed against his back. Warmth rippled out from everywhere they connected. His muscles relaxed from hard stone to simply tense.

"Okay," she said. "I guess you'll just have to change me."

"What?" Alex jerked upright.

"I'd be safest with you here at night. So if you're determined to stay out all hours, then I need to be a bear so I can fight for myself."

He spun around and searched her face. He couldn't. Wouldn't. Fuck, he'd be liable to kill her instead of doing it properly.

Her lips twitched with the ghost of a smile and he narrowed his eyes. "You're fucking with me."

"I am," she conceded with a dip of her chin. The eyes she raised to his face were big with determination. "But it stopped you spiraling, and you didn't need to go for a run so Liv, one. Alex, zero."

"More like Liv, at least two. Alex, definitely one," he smirked.

Liv shook her head in disapproval that didn't match her laugh. When she quieted, scent turned serious, and she leaned into him again. "We're going to get through this. You didn't have anyone before, but you do now."

Alex wrapped his arms around her and tucked his cheek against the top of her head. "What if we don't?" Another roar echoed through his head, wild with anguish and anger and deep resentment for the monster that made them imperfect and unworthy of Liv. "What if I always need to shift and fight a thousand times a week?"

"Then I'll invest in first aid kits." She rose up on her toes and kissed his cheek. "I see all of you and I'm not running. I expect the same."

He saw her. Grey-eyed beauty with a body to die for and a mind to think of a million reasons to keep crawling toward the next day.

Madwoman for loving a wild bear.

His madwoman.

He'd find a way to keep steady. She deserved nothing less.

CHAPTER 23

Liv frowned at the sample under the microscope. She'd started her morning with a quick look, hoping for some good news on top of the bad. Instead of living cells and a smaller area of ridges, the sample had completely deteriorated.

Balls.

Liv sat back and scowled at the microscope. Failure was more predictable than success, but that didn't make the result any easier to stomach.

Despite her best efforts, her thoughts strayed back to Alex. They should be celebrating finding their way back to each other. And while mornings spent wasting the hot water or lazing in bed were nothing short of amazing, a dark cloud still hovered over them.

It'd never really gone away.

Liv worried about him. She didn't want to repeat anything like the day in the cave. That'd he'd come back to her and seized control over his bear was nothing short of miraculous in her book, but the long hours spent in fur or twisting himself up in the sheets didn't ease her head or heart.

She didn't even mind the shifting and fighting. Alex had to blow off steam and burn off all the pent up energy. She wasn't a fighter, but she understood the need. Living among the wild beasts had given her an appreciation for the subtle differences between her and them.

No, what bothered her was that Alex still hurt. He still hunted.

She was scared of what would happen if he ever found what he searched for.

How many others felt the same way? Both from her side, and his? She was glad for all the men and women who made it through changing from human into something more without any difficulty. The others needed all the help they could get.

The biggest leap of hope since the research facility began their work had vanished overnight.

The rest of the team filtered in slowly. They winced and frowned, then went back to the notes and data. Back to the drawing board. One more test tried and failed.

Liv tried not to let it bother her, but she stayed quiet all through the morning. When the others planned for lunch in town, she dipped out at the last second and went for a quick bite in the cafeteria.

The only thing that really cheered her up were the texts she found on her phone when she took a peek. Alex started his day with an unhealthy amount of pictures of Daisy being an adorable calf, then transitioned into more and more crude and exciting promises for what he wanted to do to her once she got home.

Liv's cheeks flamed red when she pushed back into the lab, hoping for a few quiet minutes alone to get herself back into work mode.

Jenny whirled around. Liv froze, hand still on the door. They eyed each other for a long moment.

"What are you doing?" Liv asked finally. She flicked her eyes down to the large bag hanging from Jenny's shoulder.

Jenny finishing sliding an entire tube rack into the bag. "Liv. You're back early."

"What are you doing?" she repeated.

Her blood ran cold. She knew. The words were just to give herself time to think and plan. Jenny had no reason to remove samples from the lab. No one did.

Jenny was the leak.

"Dr. Franco wanted me to send these off to another facility," Jenny replied.

"Why? We're the ones analyzing everything." Fuck. Liv bounced her eyes around the room. The lab phone was too far away. She didn't know if she could flag down security before Jenny vanished. Surely she had some other way out besides the freaking front door.

She reached into her back pocket and pulled out her phone. "Let me just give him a call and—"

"Put it down." Regret and panic flashed across Jenny's face, but that didn't stop her from drawing a gun from within the bag and aiming it right at Liv.

Double fuck.

Liv slowly lowered her hand and dropped her cell to the nearest counter, keeping her eyes locked on Jenny and the gun. Betrayal stung. The accusations tossed her way were because of Jenny. Hell, the woman had probably pickpocketed her missing keycard. Jenny had taken research meant to help others and handed it over to a group determined to carry out despicable acts against anyone they deemed different.

And now she turned a gun on Liv.

They were supposed to be friends and colleagues, dammit!

"Let's be reasonable," Liv said soothingly when all she wanted to do was punch Jenny in the boob.

"I'm sorry. This is the only way." Jenny winced. "They'll hurt my family otherwise."

"You can go to the cops. They can help."

"They hurt my mom, Liv." Jenny laughed harshly. "I tried refusing, but they were prepared for that. They had someone sitting outside her home. They smacked her around and made me listen, then asked if I wanted to hear that and worse happen to my nieces and sister. They were very fucking clear about what would happen if I told anyone."

"Okay. Okay, you have to do this." She took a step aside and away from the door. Maybe Jenny wouldn't see her as such a threat if the path was clear. "I don't have to be involved. You can just let me get on my merry old way."

Every single ounce of brainpower not focused on talking her way out of trouble fired off pleas for help into the vast universe. A single person on their team returning. A lone security guard patrolling the halls. Someone taking a wrong turn at the elevator and walking past the window bank. *Please fucking find me.*

"And have you raise the alarm? Not happening." Jenny's jaw set in a firm line. "You really shouldn't have come back so soon."

Behind her, the door beeped with someone's entrance. Liv twisted, relief whipping through her at the sight of a man dressed in a security uniform. She stumbled forward, eyes wide, and pointed back to Jenny. "You have to stop her! She has a gun and is trying to steal our research!"

The man nodded reassuringly, eyes flicking to the real threat. One hand stretched out in a sign for Jenny to halt, while the other went to the weapon on his belt. "Easy, now," he said.

Liv's relief died as quickly as he snagged her wrist and spun her against his body. She struggled, but he locked her arms down. Her scream cut off with a large hand slapped over her mouth.

"The fuck?" he demanded of Jenny. "I thought you said no witnesses?"

"She wasn't supposed to be back yet. Help me tie her up." Jenny gestured to her.

"Are you crazy? She could give us up."

Liv's blood chilled. She struggled again, shaking her head in denial. Nothing budged her captor.

Alex's monster wasn't the only one in the world.

Fuck. She couldn't die. Not now. Not when she

had a sliver of happiness with him. That whiff of a future wasn't enough. She wanted more.

"We're blown as soon as we're done here," Jenny said in a low voice. She gently set the bag on a counter and reached underneath to yank out extension cords. Those, she tossed to Liv's feet. "We already have to burn the samples. That'll still be our distraction. No murder necessary."

"You think our bosses are going to be pleased if we don't meet their demands?" the security guard growled. Even so, he forced Liv into the nearest chair. Jenny arrived and stuffed a cloth into her mouth, then went back to her business. The man wrapped the cords around her painfully tight, pinning her arms to her sides. "Who are you more scared to piss off, them or the locals?"

"We're meeting them," Jenny snapped.

Jenny dumped all the samples collected from shifters into the sink, then covered them over with flammable items. Liv winced for the lost hours and potential research as Jenny pulled a lighter from her bag. One swipe of her thumb brought flames to life. She held a torn paper to the fire and dropped it into the mess.

Whoosh.

The rush of flames licked up the edges of the sink

and against the wall. Smoke billowed in a toxic, smudgy cloud.

"Let's go." Jenny looked over her shoulder once more. "Sorry," she mouthed. Then she pulled the fire alarm and scrambled out of the lab.

Liv strained against the cords with all her might. Her tongue worked at the cloth in her mouth. One moved, the other barely budged.

"Help!" she yelled.

Smoke scratched at her throat. She pushed her chair as far from the burning sink of contaminants as possible, still working against the cords wrapped around her arms and chest.

Finally, something slipped. One cord loosened enough for her to twist and turn and wiggle enough slack to slip out from under the bindings and down to the floor.

Liv dove for the nearest fire extinguisher and sprayed the flames. Once they were out, she ran through the doors and toward the stairs. She pushed through the crowd, dodging between bodies in her haste to get out of the building.

She stumbled through the doors sandwiched between others looking for an escape. Sirens blared, both from the building and in the distance. Every soul inside the facility either already milled in the parking lot or pushed to get outside. She scanned the crowd but there wasn't any sign of Jenny or her partner in crime.

Dr. Strathorn huddled with a group of security officers. Liv shoved her way through the crowd to get to them. "Jenny!" she said in a rush. "Jenny started the fire and pulled the alarm. She's been stealing information." Her eyes flicked to the others. "And one of them helped her."

Confusion furrowed Rylee's brows for a half second before she whirled around to the others. "Pull everything on Dr. Jennifer Barnes. I want her found if she's still on the grounds. Revoke all her credentials and shut her out of our systems. And find who helped her!"

The wailing sirens grew louder. Lights flashed and horns beeped to clear a path for the fire engine. Behind it, police cruisers blocked off the road to keep anyone from entering or exiting.

Rylee turned, grim focus on her face. "You stick near me. I want answers."

And Liv gave them, as much as she could. Rylee hardly let her stray more than three feet away while they bounced from authority figures and subordinates. Liv watched her direct the security team in their investigation, then worked with the local police department and Supernatural Enforcement Agency to update the situation. Even when she fielded phone calls, Liv stayed nearby in case her words were needed in another detailed report.

Finally, one of the firefighters took Rylee aside and after giving her a kiss that curled Liv's toes from ten feet away, he let them know the building was clear for regular occupation again.

Plans were put into place for the teams to go inside one by one and retrieve their belongings before being dismissed for the day. Liv was ordered to keep her phone on her in case she was needed for any other information, but was otherwise dismissed.

She marched away from the remaining crowd and eyed the line of vehicles all trying to leave at once. The second-floor teams hadn't yet been called to grab their things, so she punched a number in her phone and prodded her arm where cords had so recently held her still. Tender, but she didn't think she'd even bruise. All things considered, she was extremely lucky the day hadn't turned out worse.

A smile spread across her face as soon as Alex answered. "You won't believe the day I've had."

"Oh?" Alex clicked his tongue. A cow mooed in the background. Daisy, no doubt. "What happened?"

"Oh, just finding the source of some corporate

espionage and going all secret badass on someone. I could probably take your bear on now, that's how awesome I am. Complete with pulled fire alarms and an evacuated building."

"What?" Alex snarled. "Forget it; I'm on my way."

"I'm fine," Liv insisted. "It's nothing to worry about. I'm sure I'll be heading home before you get here, anyway."

"Dr. Olivia West?"

"Hold on. More questions, probably," she told Alex. She heard him draw a sharp breath before she lowered her phone from her ear. She turned to the voice and found a tall man standing behind her. Dark sunglasses covered his eyes. Liv made a quick inspection, looking for some badge in case there were more questions to answer. He wasn't dressed like any of the security officers, SEA agents, or local police. "Can I help you?"

"You absolutely can," he answered with a wide grin. "You know, you've been a hard one to reach."

Confusion drew her brows together. "I'm sorry?"

He gestured to the groups still waiting to get inside or trying to leave the parking lot. "With everything going on. As soon as I spotted you, you were dragged away somewhere else. Could you come this way? Just a few more questions."

"Sure." Into her phone, she said, "I'll call you right back."

"I'll be waiting," Alex answered.

She stepped around the back of a black van, expecting more of the tech she'd seen lining the insides of SEA and Bearden police vehicles alike.

Inside was empty.

Panic whipped through her just as cloth covered her nose and melted the world into darkness.

CHAPTER 24

L iv bounced awake on a wave of nausea. Her
stomach turned, and she curled in on herself.

Mistake. The movement made her head swim.
Her stomach revolted even more with the brutal
throb right behind her eyes.

"What did you do?" she said thickly.

When she found the strength to shift herself
again, Sunglasses watched her in the rearview
mirror.

She pushed past the aches in her stomach and
head. She couldn't afford to give them any energy or
thought. The van moved at a sickening, steady pace
and carried her far away from the research facility.

And away from Alex.

Eyes wide, she scrambled for her phone. Ridiculous defeat ate through her when her fingers came up empty.

And still, Sunglasses kept on driving.

Okay. No phone. A silent captor who'd grabbed her at the scene of one crime. What was the advice on cop shows? Moving to a second location lowered the chances of being found?

Liv fought another wave of nausea and sat up. The van swam again, and she wasn't sure if it was from a quick turn or simply the aftermath of whatever she'd been dosed with.

Chloroform, she thought. Not difficult to make at home, commonly dosed with a cloth.

At least the sun was still out. She couldn't have been knocked cold for very long. That bode well for a rescue.

She hoped.

"Listen," Liv croaked, "I already told everyone about Jenny. So this, whatever this is, won't help keep them a secret."

Sunglasses glanced at her again, but didn't say a word.

Maybe Jenny had a change of heart. Or her mysterious bosses wanted to tie up loose ends. Maybe she was taken to send a message.

Fucking hell, she wasn't in a damn mob movie. This was her life!

"They're gone, anyway. In the wind. Poofed out of existence." Liv drew a shaky breath to keep her voice steady. "Taking me isn't going to help anyone."

The air thickened around her and Sunglasses growled a low warning. "You talk too much."

"I'm just trying to be reasonable," she said. "I'm pointless. In fact, taking me back can only help you."

"You're far from pointless. You serve a bigger purpose."

Chills ran up and down her spine at the words.

Sunglasses touched a thick finger to his shades and lowered them a fraction of an inch. Bright green eyes glowed in the reflection. "What do you think will hurt him more? Killing you or seeing you become just like us?"

Liv's face drained of blood. Her stomach turned again, but chloroform sickness had nothing to do with it.

Alex's maker. His monster stared at her.

And she was trapped in a van with him.

No doubt he had some terrible plan for her that would make Alex suffer even more. She wanted no part of his twisted scheme.

"He'll find you. He'll make you pay for everything you've done."

"Maybe." He grinned savagely. "It'll be too late for you, though."

Not if she had anything to say about that.

Liv eyed the latch to the back door. He hadn't tied her up, perhaps hoping she'd stay out longer. That was the danger of playing chemistry at home. Sometimes the results didn't go as expected.

She was thinking of everything except what she intended. She had to. Otherwise her brain might revolt and keep her locked safely in place where she waited for her fate.

Fuck that.

Liv lunged for the door. Her fingers scrabbled at the latch until one side flung open. Road sped away from her and turned her stomach. The rush of air was loud in her ears.

She closed her eyes and tumbled out.

Her shoulder hit the ground and she rolled. Awkwardly. She ignored the biting pain that twisted through her. She could deal with a busted shoulder and bruises all over her body. Those injuries meant she still lived.

She eyed the road ahead and behind, then the trees next to the road. In the far distance, a car barreled toward them, but she wouldn't reach it before her captor caught up to her. Still, she sprinted for it, wildly waving her arms.

Fuck. Stupid. She'd played her hand too soon.

The van slammed to a stop and reversed after her. She jumped off the road and onto the grass.

Sunglasses yanked the wheel and pulled to a stop inches from her. The driver's side door creaked open.

Her only hope was the car's driver spotting her and calling for help before she was overtaken.

Liv ran for the trees.

ALEX LEANED on his forearms and clasped his hands together. The plastic chair underneath him was uncomfortable compared to the cot in the holding cell, but he wasn't at the police station for some drunk and disorderly charge.

He watched the two teams bustle around like chickens with their heads sliced off. The local Bearden cops wanted to prove something to the SEA agents strutting around. The SEA contingent had sticks up their asses and didn't want to rely on local yokels for help with either case they all worked.

His bear roared, and he clasped his hands together harder. Claws bit into his palms. Better that than letting the beast take his skin and tear into each and every person who wouldn't put aside their bullshit and find his fucking mate.

He should have known something was wrong. One comment. Just a handful of words strung together. Those had been the tell. She wasn't easy to get to? No fucking shit. That'd been by design.

But the monster hunted. He'd waited patiently and took his shot when an opportunity presented itself.

Alex had arrived at the research facility in record time, dialing Liv's phone every time it went to voicemail. Sloan had still been there, helping clear the building of employees while others worked to find the ones Liv mentioned. He couldn't even remember the words Sloan shouted at him when he tore through the parking lot and began searching for Liv.

The world had turned red when he spotted her cell on the side of the road. He'd recognize the black case with a sparkly skull on the back even if her scent hadn't been all over the device.

Another roar. Another tightening of his jaw and his fists to keep the beast locked inside. Two drops of blood splattered to the floor at his feet.

"Easy," Ethan muttered at his side.

Power washed over him and tried to soothe him. Tried, and failed.

But he kept to his skin. He would be more of use on two feet than the wild and unmanageable bear on four.

If there was any progress made. Alex drew in a big breath and let it go slowly. Silently, he went over every detail once more.

No one saw her leave. No one spotted her being taken.

The security footage was fucking useless. Nothing existed on the tape because of whatever other scheme had been pulled that day. His word and her phone sitting on the ground were the only clues to go on, and neither were any damn help.

Bearden cops and SEA agents put out the word right on the heels of the first breaking story and promised to keep him updated.

So he waited with his alpha at his side and tried not to feel like he was being babysat and watched for any potential freak-out.

Sloan peeled away from another group and stepped through the waist-high swinging doors separating the bullpen from the waiting area. She looped her thumbs through her belt loops and shot him a pitying look that grated.

"There's no reason for you to stick around. We'll give you any updates we get."

Ethan canted his head. "We'll stay."

Sloan pressed her lips together. "Look—"

"We're not leaving." Ethan rose to his feet. "You're doing your job; I get that. Alex is doing his. We'll stay out of the way, but we're here. We're in this. We're bringing her home."

Useless. He felt fucking useless.

His mate was in danger and all he could do was sit around and wait for someone else to find her. He should have locked her in a deep mountain bunker the first moment he caught her scent and his maker's in the same thousand-mile stretch.

And what damn good did it do to have personal connections with the damn Supernatural Enforcement Agency when she tried to send them home?

A growl rattled in his throat. Both Ethan and Sloan darted eyes to him, but he didn't move.

"We're staying," Ethan said after a second.

Sloan dipped her chin and moved back through the swinging doors.

"Really think it's a good idea to fuck with someone who can shoot you?" Ethan muttered.

Alex glared and kept silent. He didn't care who he pissed off. He'd wreck a thousand days if it meant Liv's safety.

Nothing else to do, he picked through the day's events again. Each repetition firmed up his memories, but didn't give him any clearer of a view. He still didn't know where Liv had been taken or the face of the one who'd nabbed her. Fuck, six years and that clipped tone in the background was the first time he'd heard the bastard's voice.

All he had was a fleeting scent and a growing need to fight. His bear paced through his head, swiping at him with claws. *Move,* the beast urged. *Find her.*

Sendings pushed into his head that he quickly waved away. He couldn't focus on those happy images when a sick, oily sense of loss filled his stomach.

A wave of renewed activity rolled through the station. Heads came together as word hopped from group to group. The murmurings reached a crescendo as local cops maneuvered to the back of the station and strapped themselves into gear. The agents pushed their way out the door and engines sputtered to life.

Sloan again pushed her way out of the bullpen

and into the waiting area. Fierce light brightened her eyes. "There was a report of a woman throwing herself out of a van south of here."

Alex perked up and spoke for the first time since Ethan appeared at his side at the research facility and forced him to quit yelling like a madman. "Was it her?"

Sloan shook her head. "We don't know. A group is heading that way now."

He rose to his feet. She pressed her lips together. A shake of her head came with a burst of frustration in her scent. "Stay to the back. I'm not filing extra paperwork if either of you get shot."

He was out the door before she finished, with Ethan right on his heels.

The parking lot filled with bodies making beelines for vehicles. Lights flashed to life with the wail of sirens. Cruisers and SUVs peeled out of the parking lot and raced down the road.

Faster, Alex urged. His bear rumbled a growled agreement.

Time slowed to a crawl even as the caravan barreled forward. They burst out of the mountains and into hill country to the song of sirens. The wails carried them down the sparsely populated road between the enclave and the rest of human civilization.

A black van sat on the side of the road. One of the back doors hung open, as did the driver's. The engine still ran.

Just ahead was a small car. An elderly man held the shaking shoulders of a woman. His wife, Alex assumed. He didn't hear anything over the buzz of voices, but the man pointed into the trees.

Alex was out of the truck as soon as Ethan pulled to the side of the road. Cops and agents scurried all over the scene and commanded him to stop, but he didn't listen. Fury and worry struck him deaf and blind to anything but finding Liv.

That bastard. He choked on the scent of him as soon as he got near the van. Liv's intoxicating smell was nearly snuffed out under the slimy stench of his maker.

Ten feet from the van, though, the bastard switched direction. Liv's was the only one that entered the trees directly in front of him.

Alex felt sick. His maker hunted his mate.

"Did any other cars pass? We need to know if the other one was picked up," someone said in the background.

He wasn't. Alex stared away from the road and

yanked his shirt over his head. Two paths were as clear as day, but he only concerned himself with one. He had Liv's scent in his nose. That trail was the most important one in the world.

He kicked out of his boots and shucked his pants. Objections rose as soon as he was noticed. Fuck 'em. They could tranq him if they had a problem with what he intended.

He was going after Liv.

His muscles snapped and his bones cracked. Fur slid out of his pores and he fell to his paws. His bear ripped out of him and, nose gathering Liv's scent, he tore after his mate.

Her path was easy to follow. Thick with fear, she dug her nails into his fur and led him on. Between thick trunks and thinner ones. Through prickly brush. Liv ran as far and as fast as possible while he'd been sitting on his ass waiting for some small word of hope.

Alex roared at the first tinge of blood at the exact spot his maker's scent crossed with Liv's.

A roar answered him, coming from behind. Ethan. His alpha. He let him lead and didn't try to stop him, but he was there nonetheless. Watching. Waiting. Alex knew the stakes. He'd seen the vicious power of a mate denied. Ethan, Hunter, Lorne, they'd all been through the destruction of nearly watching their other half torn away. None of them were half as fucked up as him.

Ethan would keep him from going off the deep end, even if it meant Alex's death.

He pushed forward, following the metallic scent of blood and odor of fear. Those told a story, as did the stench of the bastard crossing paths, then vanishing into the trees again. His maker played with her.

Alex raked claws down a tree trunk to burn off an inch of fury. Liv needed him.

At the bottom of the slope and covered over in leaves and other debris, was a body.

Fuck. *Fuck.* By the bloody Broken and all the gods in the sky. Fucking piece of shit psychotic asshole!

Alex tore down the slope as fast as possible, shifting along the way. He lunged the last few steps and skidded to her side on his knees.

Shallow breath reached his ears as he pulled Liv into his lap. Her pants were torn and hung ragged. Blood smeared over her arms and exposed legs. The scent of fur mingled with the tangy, exotic base.

Bitten. The wounds had mostly closed and left behind silvery scars just like his own.

Alex squeezed his eyes closed. He had her, and he still might lose her.

She had others. She had him. And that still might not make a difference to the unruly beast unwillingly placed in her middle.

And that was if she survived the change. Women fared better, but he'd never wanted to put that to the test.

Behind him, others crashed through the woods.

Ahead of him, a branch snapped.

Alex whipped his attention to the bear stepping out between thick tree trunks. Bright green eyes focused on him.

His grief transformed into pure rage. He'd found a sliver of happiness with someone who understood him. He was a wild creature and likely wouldn't ever change, but she didn't care. She still wanted to be with him.

And that fucking prick wanted to trample all over his new life. He'd already made the journey to his mate longer than it had to be. He wouldn't take her from him again.

Fuck being a decent person. Screw keeping himself steady.

Alex let his bear rip out of him with a savage roar and charged.

He was thankful for every fight he'd ever provoked or launched himself into. They built him up for the exact moment he needed to defend his mate.

He crashed into the other bear hard enough to shake the ground under their feet. The tremors didn't stop him in the slightest.

Paws slapped. Claws raked. He roared and bit, backed off and circled. He leaped forward at any sign of weakness or hesitation. There was no testing, no waiting for a feint. He thundered past all the bastard's defenses with an explosion of rage six years in the making.

He hurt Liv. He stole her choice and forced a rabid animal into her. For that alone, Alex wanted him to cease living.

Blood wet his tongue and coated his claws. His maker still roared and spun and attacked, showing no sign of slowing. Alex refused to give up. Wouldn't comprehend the idea. Not while the bastard that hurt him and his mate still drew breath.

Blow after blow. Fangs snapped in his shoulders, against his ear. He paid them back with raking claws and crunching jaws. Every time he twisted around and blocked the other bear's path from Liv, renewed strength and determination dumped into his veins.

He would keep her safe.

He rose up on hind legs and swung heavy paws into his maker. The bastard huffed and whined as claws dragged down his back. Alex dropped to four paws and ripped into him, tearing with teeth until a final shake of his head brought the fight to an end with a resounding *crack.*

Alex stepped back and let the body of his monster fall to the ground, finally, thankfully, put to rest.

Fur melted from him as he whipped back around. His shape shimmered and four legs became two. Others streamed around him, but he only had eyes for Liv.

He dropped down next to her again and drew her back into his lap. "Come on, Liv. You have to wake up. Give me some sign you're in there."

She'd pulled him out of the darkness. He'd do the same for her. If he had to sit by her night and day until her body accepted the changes, he'd do it. He'd talk himself hoarse to keep her grounded in this world.

"I can't do this without you. I was barely hanging on before you waltzed back into my life." The words pushed past his lips, soft and powerful all at once. His honest truth. "I need you. I need us. I don't care if that makes me selfish. You can't die on me. I won't survive without you."

Claws slashed at his middle. His bear wanted to murder his maker all over again, then find whoever was in charge of writing their fate and do the same. There wasn't a shred of decency on this side of the veil if he lost Liv, found her, and lost her all over again.

Her eyes flickered open, then closed again. A tiny smile played across her lips. "You have me."

Alex cupped her head and held her close while he nodded. His heart stuttered to a start again, matching the rapid pace of hers.

He had her. Fate and wild bears be damned.

CHAPTER 25

Alex wiped a hand across his forehead and settled his Stetson back on his head. He forced a grin and waved at the last car to pull away from the ranch. Tension crawled up his spine and tingled in the cheeks he finally relaxed.

Fuck, he needed a drink.

A punch landed on his arm. He jumped and growled his displeasure at Hunter. The man's grin broadened and Alex knew he was about to be pissed off. Still, he ground his teeth together and tried to play nice. A mated man couldn't fly off the handle every three seconds and brawl from sunup to sundown.

"Gonna need you to take over both rides booked for tomorrow," Ethan said as he exited the barn.

Alex scuffed the toe of his boot against a clod in the dirt. Instead of falling apart, he unearthed a bit of rock. He frowned as he worked at it, digging until it rolled loose.

"Sounds fine," he grumbled between gritted teeth.

Lorne regarded him with something close to curiosity on his face. Hunter and Jesse wore matching grins that Alex wanted to wipe off their stupid faces. Ethan folded his arms over his chest and leaned against a fence post, letting whatever happened play out like his favorite television show.

Fuckers. All of them.

He'd tried to stay on his best behavior since Liv was...

Alex swallowed back bile that turned his stomach. He could barely think about the day without wanting to bleed the world.

And that was wrong.

He had everything he wanted. His mate was safe. His maker was dead. He should be twirling in a field of flowers and shitting out rainbows.

But his bear's need for brawls hadn't slackened in the slightest. The teasing that swirled in his clan's scents made him want to snap at them all. If he couldn't keep his shit together when the world served him up slices of happiness and satisfaction on a silver fucking platter, how could he possibly think he'd be a good mate to Liv?

He definitely didn't want to talk about it with any of the men watching him.

"Cheer up, man," Hunter said with a straight face. "I'm sure she's seen your tiny pecker before. If she can get over that disappointment, she can live with being mated to you."

"No marks yet," Lorne grunted.

Damn truth speaker. Alex glowered in his direction. Did everyone fucking gossip about him when his back was turned?

"Liv probably decided to ditch him. I mean, wouldn't you?" Hunted prodded again.

His bear shoved forward with a snarl. Alex yanked the beast back before his bones cracked. Sendings flashed through his mind of all the pain he wanted to inflict on the other man, but he kept himself in check.

Barely.

Besides, he had long term plans in place to get back at the man for some slight he hardly remembered. The payoff would be worth letting a few more remarks slide.

"Maybe he doesn't know where to stick it." Hunter

made a circle with one hand and poked a finger through.

Alex snarled. He picked up the rock and hurled it at Hunter's chest. "Just because your mate needs to take care of herself while you're snoring away next to her, doesn't mean I leave my woman unsatisfied."

Hunter yelped at the impact and then laughed. "There's the Alex we love to hate!"

"Fucking finally." Ethan thanked the sky with open hands and a relieved look. "We were wondering how long until you snapped back at us. This weirdness has got to stop."

"You're wild, man. A please and thank you are nice changes, but that smile is creeping out the tourists," Jesse teased. "And you haven't once tried to fight us."

"Fuck you all," Alex growled. "I'm trying to be a decent man—"

"There's your first mistake," Hunter said under his breath. "Thinking you're a decent anything."

Alex rounded on him and threw a punch into his stomach with a roar. They scuffled, both landing blows on one another. The edge of his anger melted away with each punch and curse that passed between his lips.

"All right," Ethan said. "Break it up. We don't want to send him back home bruised and bloody."

Hunter grabbed him one last headlock. Alex shoved himself out of the way and grinned when the other man hit the ground.

"Give our best to Liv." Ethan tipped the brim of his hat, mouth twitching. "Maybe you'll figure out where to stick it."

Alex growled and narrowed his eyes. He stalked off toward his home, both fingers raised in a final salute to the assholes of his clan.

Fuckers always knew how to ruin a good thing.

Liv's scent hit him square in the face as soon as he yanked open his door and stomped inside. Doubts piled up as soon as he did. He'd been trying to be better, but failed at that.

Wild, they called him. Yeah. Unpredictable and brash, with a beast under his skin. And he still hadn't been able to keep Liv safe.

His bear rolled through him in agitation and denial. There it was. The biggest, jagged piece of the whole damn puzzle. He was still fucked up. Why would she tie herself to that for the rest of her life?

Alex scowled and dropped his Stetson to the counter. He went straight for the fridge, cracked open a beer, and took a long pull from the bottle before starting toward the bedroom, intending to jump straight in the shower. He wanted another attempt to wash his sins clean before he tried putting words to the murky thoughts filling his head.

Instead, he paused at the door and stared.

Liv convalesced in his den. In his bed. The sight of her there, in nothing but a black tank top and panties, should have made him happy and hard. She was his mate. His bear certainly loved her scent slowly filling every inch of the place.

Her flushed cheeks and bright eyes were a stark reminder of how he'd failed her.

In the end, his monster still won. Liv had an animal that'd soon be unleashed on the world.

An open notebook rested across her lap, but Liv's attention was on the vial of blood she drew from her own arm. With help from her coworkers, she'd turned her side of the bed into a home lab. They'd even left her with a mini-fridge to store samples between their visits. Labels were scattered over the nightstand, along with a thermometer and small device that she regularly wrapped around her wrist to measure her blood pressure.

Alex leaned against the door frame. "Be careful. You're not going to have any blood left."

She flicked him a glance. "We haven't had a chance to see the process in action. This is such a rare opportunity. I'm not going to waste it."

"Aren't there rules about turning yourself into the science experiment?"

"We're in the wild west of progress. There are no rules. And... done." Before he could object, Liv hopped out of bed long enough to settle the tube among the others in the mini-fridge. She stored or disposed of supplies with quick precision, then slid a bandage over the puncture site.

Not much blood to bandage, Alex mused. He took another pull from his bottle. If she followed his same path, she had another day before her inner animal demanded to be released.

Liv climbed back into bed and looked at him expectantly. "Now, can I have that?"

"You want this?" Playing dumb, he pointed at himself.

She scrunched her nose, eyes sparkling with mischief. One look, and he felt tension melt off his shoulders. He breathed easier around her.

His mate. Gorgeous, perfect mate. She made him want to be better.

So what if he wasn't a perfect gentleman all the time? At least he tried.

"Hit it. Quit it." She almost kept a straight face. Almost. "That bottle is way more interesting."

"This one. Right here?" He tapped his finger on the bottle and pushed off the door frame. Her scent and smile had him by the balls and dragged him forward. "The one I'm about to drink?"

"What would it take for you to share it with me?" Her lips hitched up in a lopsided smile as her fingers grabbed the hem of her shirt. "Maybe a little skin?"

"What are you willing to pay? If I'm going to get reamed out for going against the doctor's orders..." Alex planted a knee between her thighs and took a long swig out of the bottle, keeping his eyes fixed on hers.

"Luckily *this* doctor says it's fine." She dragged her shirt up to expose an inch of her stomach.

He landed his second knee on the other side of her leg. "Haven't you drawn too much blood? You're practically drained."

"Just makes me a cheap date."

Alex leaned forward and kissed her stomach. Her scent swirled in his nose. Sweet and exotic and tempting even with the new notes of fur added to the mix. He'd kept his hands off her since settling her under the blankets, but his bear rode him harshly to complete the bond. Even working himself to exhaustion hadn't killed the urge to sink between her thighs and press fangs into her skin.

But she needed time to recover.

Time to pick him of her own will.

He didn't want life or death to be involved. He wanted it to be man and woman, just them, two people coming together as they should have years before.

Liv's fingers threaded through his hair and she hissed when he pressed the cold bottle to her navel.

"Still want this?"

"In my mouth."

He snorted and nosed the hem of her shirt higher. "Oh, I have something you can put in your mouth."

"You've been avoiding me." She twisted her fingers in his hair and pulled him away from her body. "We haven't talked about things."

Alex sat up with a growl and swept his hair back with his hand. "Nothing to talk about," he said in a gruff voice.

"Strongly disagree."

Liv rose up on her knees and pressed herself against his back. Her arms wrapped around his chest and her chin rested on his shoulder. Warmth coursed through him. Contentment. A soft growl rumbled out of him before he could lock down the noise.

All the doubts rushed back.

He'd failed her. He hadn't kept her safe. That bastard still took advantage of a crisis and stole her from him. Sheer luck gave away her location. Alex hated the number of points where he could have lost her forever, but he couldn't push those thoughts away.

What if no one had been driving down the road when she jumped? What if she landed wrong and broke her damn fool neck? The silvery scars on her arms and legs matched his own; their maker hadn't been gentle. Any one of those bites could have hit an artery and drained her life into the dirt. He could have fought and lost and left her to her fate.

Liv stroked a hand down the back of his head. The touch quieted a growl he hadn't been aware rumbled away in his throat.

"You have to let me in." She turned her head and kissed his cheek.

Her choice. She'd picked him before. Was it too much to think she'd do so again? The dark cloud hanging over him rumbled and threatened to crash lightning, but there was a break in the coverage. Sun shined down on the woman seated behind him.

He couldn't give her up. She belonged to him.

He rolled her back to the mattress and nuzzled the crook of her neck. She gasped sharply, thighs slamming together. His bear surged forward with a press of fangs in his gums and a flash of sendings almost too fast to process. Alex didn't need to see the individual images. The impression was enough.

His mate needed to be claimed.

"You need to know what you're getting into."

Amusement laced her scent. "I have a fair idea."

"I don't have anything to offer you. You'd be better off with literally anyone else on the planet." He tongued his teeth and rolled his face to meet her eyes. "I'm rough, Liv. I still want to fight all the damn time." The others prodded him into showing that weakness. "And I don't want to let you go."

She was quiet for a long moment. Too long. His bear started pacing through his head before she squeezed him tightly and said, "Then don't."

He drew her wrists above her head and kissed her throat. Right there. A growl rattled in his chest. He wanted to claim her right where he placed his lips.

"I hurt you before thinking I was protecting you," he raised his head and breathed against her lips. "You were still hurt because of me."

"Then you fought for me and brought me back home." She leaned up, as much as she could, and nipped his lower lip. Hooded eyes watched him when she relaxed back down. "I don't care how wild you are. I want to be your mate."

The words stunned him. They were exactly what he wanted to hear, hoped she'd say, but they still brought his mind to a standstill.

Perfect woman. Too smart and brave for her own good. He looked forward to a lifetime of her running circles around him.

"You're hurt," he said carefully.

"I'm healed and bored of staying in bed all day. Don't make me wait any longer."

Alex dragged a line of kisses across her jaw. "I like hearing you beg," he answered, his voice dropping to the pitch of pure gravel.

A flicker of green swirled in the grey of her eyes. The color matched his and their maker's. Unnervingly beautiful. She turned something and someone terrible into beauty. He hadn't been in time to save her, but maybe she turned up at the right moment to save him.

Alex rolled to his knees long enough to drag her upright and strip her of her tank top. Her hands reached for the hem of his shirt and dragged it over his head. Fingers trailed gently across his stomach and over his chest. Down his arms to the silvery scars that marked him as a bitten shifter. He'd hated them for so long, then wore them as a badge of stubborn pride. Never had they felt part of him until that moment.

Liv brought his arm between them and followed the path of one silvery line with her tongue, eyes watching him the entire time. "Mine," she said.

Sweet arousal hit the air and made his mouth water for a taste. Alex growled and cupped a breast and leaned into her, bending her back down to the mattress.

"Beg for me, Liv," he ordered. He thumbed her nipple and lowered his head, within striking distance of taking her into his mouth. His breath bathed her skin and raised goose bumps up and down her arms. "Tell me what you want."

"You."

The arch of her back pushed the swell of her breast to his mouth. He teased her with a lick, then sucked the stiff peak between his lips, his other hand cupping her other breast. He switched between the two, laving and teasing until her chest heaved with panted breaths.

Not to be outdone, Liv rolled her hips against his thick erection.

Their bodies moved together like they were made for each other. Her hips pulsed into his, he ground down between her legs. Hiss, groan. Suckle, moan.

"More," she whimpered.

Alex slid a hand down her stomach and into the front of her panties, fingers diving deep into her slick heat. He wanted to take his time, work her up, but the broken noises trickling out of her throat drove him up the wall with need. She looked so fucking sexy with her dark hair spread around her face and her eyes rolling closed. More red spread over her cheeks as he pumped into her, hooking his fingers just right to catch that sweet spot inside that made her writhe against him.

"Love how you sound, baby," he growled, stroking into her again and again.

He didn't wait for her next begging command. He trailed a path of biting kisses down her ribs and over her hips and tore away the thin strip of fabric keeping him from her. His bear rode him hard to taste more of her.

He dipped his head between her thighs, shoulders spreading her wide open. Liv's hands fluttered against her sides as he inhaled sharply and licked a path around her clit. Her breath turned ragged when he pulled her between his lips, still pumping fingers into her heat.

She was everything. His mate. His life. She didn't shy away from the dark parts once she understood them. She accepted every part of him and made him a better person.

She belonged with him. He wanted to complete their connection. Needed to feel her right at the brink when he marked her as his mate.

"Alex!"

Liv arched into him and threaded her fingers into his hair. Feral sounds poured out of her mouth. Her hips bucked against him until he growled and slammed his hands down on her thighs, holding her steady. He licked and sucked mercilessly, groaning as her sweetness hit his tongue. She exploded around him, sharp scream ripping through the air and his restraint.

He needed her. *Now.*

ALEX'S JEANS hit the ground with a thud. Then he was back between her thighs, driving deep into her and riding through her release. Her body shook at the sudden invasion, rolling another orgasm through her right on the heels of the first and stealing her breath.

His cock slid home, filling her completely. Her body stretched to fit him and Liv buried her face in the crook of his neck.

Her heart burst wide open at their joining. She felt nearly complete, almost whole, part of something bigger for the first time in her entire life. This was what fate intended for her from the very beginning, and she was finally nearing those final steps.

He broke her heart once before and now he put the pieces back together. The years between, she'd always found a way to keep her walls up and everyone else on the outside. She'd been better alone, she'd lied to herself. He'd torn that idea to shreds long even before the run for her life. She wanted a way in, now. She wouldn't give up on him for the world.

Liv hooked her ankles around Alex. Her mate. Something soft brushed against her mind and she grinned. Her thought, the spark of an inner animal, she didn't know. The word was perfect, though. That was all that mattered.

He pushed himself up on his hands, black curls

falling into his bright green eyes. Liv smoothed his hair back and rose up on her elbows to meet his mouth.

"Tell me what you want," he breathed against her lips.

Goose bumps tingled to life up and down her arms.

"Mate me," she whispered back. "Make me yours."

Alex retreated and slammed home, jaw tight. "Say it again."

His eyes caught hers. So bright. Trouble swirled in the green. Mischief. Determination. All the parts of him she adored combined together in a heated look that stole her breath.

"Yours. Always." Liv cupped his cheek and dragged him down into a kiss.

He retreated again and drove into her, deeper than before. Every sliding thrust dragged against her skin and sparked her nerves. Her middle churned with the vast need he implanted in her, the desire to seal herself to him for the rest of their days.

Soft fur brushed against her mind again and a ragged growl tore out of her throat.

"Fuck, baby," he groaned. He nipped at her neck. "Let me hear that again."

She met him stroke for stroke. His hands slid

over her skin, his fingers dug into her hips. His thrusts sped up, shortened, and he drove into her deeper and harder still. Liv panted and moaned under him, taking everything he gave until fire burned in her veins.

"Need you, Liv." Deep desire coated his words. Smug satisfaction curved up his lips in a smirk. And love... love shined in his eyes.

All she could do was nod.

The low rumble of his voice added another stroking layer to all the other sensations building inside her. A need for more still buzzed in her head, making her feel a different sort of fire than her fast approaching release. Her head swam. Her vision wavered. She needed something...

"More," she moaned, tilting her head to the side.

Alex brought his lips down against her throat. Teeth and tongue and lips burned against her skin with the biting, sucking kisses he trailed up the column of her neck.

"Tell me what you want," he growled in her ear.

Her answer was the same as before. Notes of desperation colored her tone. "Mate me. Make me yours."

Her hips danced under him as he continued thrusting deep into her. Lights sparked behind her eyelid with every blink. Pleasure bubbled in her blood, rising up with the impending combustion.

Liv threw her head back with a scream. Faint pain pierced her senses, followed by a bright surge of bliss.

More.

Liv turned her head. Her lips mouthed against his skin. And she bit.

Alex roared. His hand slammed into the bed next to her head. He locked his hips against hers and flooded her with warmth.

They both shook when he eased away from her shoulder and pressed his forehead against hers. Too many words swirled in her head, none of them more right than simply mingling their breath at that moment. Liv wrapped her arms around her mate's neck and sighed with contentment.

Wild man. Her man.

Her mate.

With him, she'd never know what to expect. And she couldn't wait to see what'd he'd do next.

EPILOGUE

L iv dug her hands into the dirt and sucked down another breath. Afternoon sun beat down on her back. Her hair hung in her face, each strand feeling like a thread of fire. Her skin itched worse than she ever remembered while also feeling strangely tight.

She logged the details while the sense of something more pushed outward across every inch of her body.

She knew the mechanics of what to expect, but knowing didn't prepare her in the slightest for experiencing.

"Stop thinking so much," Alex growled with rebuke. "Don't fight her. Close your eyes and let go."

Easy for him to say.

The grumble in her head came with affection. She'd spent the night and day in her mate's arms, alternating between renewing their bond over and over and devouring everything he put in front of her.

The sense of something else inside her grew with every passing hour until Alex had stiffened and thumbed open her eyes, then ordered her outside.

Liv dragged down another breath and squeezed closed her eyes. The darkness behind her lids morphed or maybe dragged her further into herself, she didn't know which. But slowly, she realized she wasn't alone.

She turned inside herself and faced off against a giant bear.

Black fur covered her from front to back without a speck of color anywhere. A large head swiveled toward Liv and glowing green eyes latched onto hers. The beast stepped forward with pure confidence and shoved Liv out of the way.

The moment she let go, fur pressed against her mind.

Pain started in her fingers and toes and worked its way up her limbs and into her spine. Sharp cracks entered the air, then she was wrenched away from time and space.

When she plopped back into herself, she was a bear.

Liv stumbled to her paws, twisting around and around to try getting a better look at herself. Black fur. Four paws. Thick legs. Check, check, check.

Another smattering of pops and cracks jerked her attention to Alex. His form shifted and then his inner animal stood before her.

He lunged at her and she ran.

Wind rustled through her fur. Her claws dug into the earth. Sights and sounds pressed down around her, but the scents gave the world a whole new dimension.

Liv slammed to a stop and shoved her nose against the ground. Grass. Sweet grass and flowers with drops of water and loads of pollen. The air was thick with scents that made her stomach rumble.

Nearby, a cow loudly mooed.

Alex slowed next to her and rubbed his head against her shoulder. Reassurance and encouragement to keep on moving and figuring out her new self.

With another bump of his head, he chuffed at her and turned toward a group of trees. He stretched himself tall against one and dragged his claws down the bark, leaving a mark for all to see.

Liv copied him, rising up on her back legs and balancing against the strong trunk. Her claws dug into the wood just as he'd done. She pressed harder and softer, learning just what sort of damage she could inflict.

Important, that. The life of a shifter wasn't entirely peaceful, as she'd learned firsthand.

A growl rattled in her throat. She turned toward the roaming cattle and startled them with a roar.

The noise was a challenge to anyone who'd try to part her from her mate again. A demand to back off and never show their face. And a promise to stick by him for all her days.

No one would tear their world asunder again.

Not the asshole without a name or identification that ruined Alex's life for six long years and completely changed her own. Their maker was a crazed mystery who'd been handed the ultimate price for his crimes.

Not the accomplices to hunter cells seeking to eradicate supernatural kind. Jenny and her bogus security guard were still on the run, but the serum team was determined to redouble their efforts, using Liv's samples as the start of their new research.

Alex shoved his nose against her neck. A growl rumbled out of him, but he didn't smell sharp or angry in the slightest. Liv sank into the relaxed feeling of him standing so close.

When he moved away, she followed.

He led her over Black Claw lands, letting her pick up different scent trails and following them until another snagged her attention. Along fences, chasing cows, near and far from the houses that sat in the very center of the territory. He introduced her to her lands, her clan, and her new life.

There was no one else she'd rather have by her side. The afternoon was perfect.

She wasn't sure how long they spent in fur. Hours. Long enough for the sun to sink close to the horizon and streak oranges into the blue sky.

Liv's ears twitched as they neared the houses again. The noise grew with a chorus of voices and laughter once they crested a final hill. Down in the middle of the yard between the main house and barn was the entire clan.

She rumbled her surprise and Alex nudged her forward, smelling amused.

Tansey and Joss directed where to place the spread of food on tables dragged from storage somewhere. Ethan and Hunter begrudgingly followed orders while Sloan, Lorne, and Jesse peppered them with suggestions and insults.

After one particularly insulting volley, Hunter slammed the tray of food in his hands to the table, grabbed a chicken wing, and threw it at Jesse. The other man simply shrugged and bit into the wing, raising a middle finger as thanks.

Liv laughed—chuffed—and stumbled to a startled stop. Alex swung his head into her side and urged her forward.

She was part of their exclusive club now. Her new instincts threatened to overwhelm her with happy pride.

Joss turned, her hand on a belly that seemed to grow larger every day. "There you are," she greeted with an exasperated look over her shoulder. "Hurry up and change so we can properly welcome you to the clan. We might not have any food left!"

Liv turned with Alex for their hut, glad for the privacy. Shifting back to her human side went easier than becoming a bear, but she still struggled and needed several long minutes before her legs stopped feeling like jelly and she could stomach putting clothes against her skin.

Finally dressed and back on two feet, Alex sifted hands into her hair and gently kissed her lips. "You ready for this?"

She nodded and slipped her hand into his. "Let's do it."

The activity stopped as soon as they stepped back into the group. She didn't know who was the first to clap, but they were welcomed into the middle of the group to the sound. Alex stayed by her side as Ethan stepped forward and crushed her into a hug.

"Welcome to the clan, Liv," he rumbled. He pointed at Alex. "You make sure this one behaves."

"Not likely," she chuckled.

One after the other, they all stepped forward to give her a hug and welcome her to the clan. There was more to the greeting, she realized after Ethan. They were learning her scent, just as she was figuring out how to pick them apart by her nose alone.

Joss was the last to give her a hug. "Watch out for Hunter," she warned.

Before Liv could ask why, the door banged open. The other man careened back outside, frustrated fury written all over his face as he waved a picture frame in the air.

"Alex!" Hunter shouted.

Joss sank her head into her hands and sighed. "Here we go."

Alex snickered quietly and Liv turned. "What did you do?" she demanded sternly.

Wide-eyed innocence didn't cover the lie in his scent. "Wasn't me."

"'Wasn't me. Wasn't me.'" Hunter stomped off the porch and made a face. "Fuck you, dickhole, I can smell your stank all over the wood!"

"Must smell pretty nice, then," Liv called back and popped a chip into her mouth. Joss jabbed her in the side with an elbow. Tansey and Sloan outright laughed.

Hunter narrowed his eyes at her and shook a finger. "I know this is your shifting party and clan welcome, but don't take his damn side."

"Well, what did he do?"

"Replaced pictures of Hunter," Joss started.

"With that damn cow of his!" Hunter shook the frame again. "Every last one of them! Cow heads, cow asses, fuck, even damn cow *shit*! My wedding picture is this beautiful woman," he gestured to Joss, who struggled to keep her smile contained, "standing next to a giant turd!"

Liv bit her lip to hold back her laughter. She leaned closer to Joss. "How long did that take?"

"Weeks, I think. I noticed the first one days ago."

Alex glanced at her with a raised eyebrow. She knew what question he asked.

Liv waved him on. "Get it over with."

Alex slammed a hand to his chest. "I don't know what you're talking about."

"Don't play dumb with me. I'm not waiting for you to eat."

The other mates exchanged glances. "Us, either," Joss proclaimed.

Grinning, Alex threw his arms wide and squared off against Hunter. "Figured your mate would want something nice to look at for a change."

Liv laughed. He wasn't perfect even on a good day. But he was more relaxed than ever. There was still a wildness to him, but his shoulders didn't seem as tense and he was freer with proper, genuine smiles instead of clenched teeth and sarcasm.

Hunter's bear ripped out of him with a roar. Alex's followed half a second later. The two beasts crashed into one another while the rest of the clan went about their business like the brawl was nothing out of the ordinary.

No, Alex wasn't perfect. But he was hers.

They were all hers.

Liv smiled to herself and joined her new clan.

ABOUT THE AUTHOR

Cecilia Lane grew up in a what most call paradise, but she insists is humid hell. She escaped the heat with weekly journeys to the library, where she learned the basics of slaying dragons, magical abilities, and grand adventures.

When it became apparent she wouldn't be able to travel the high seas with princes or party with rock star vampires, Cecilia hunkered down to create her own worlds filled with sexy people in complicated situations. She now writes with the support of her own sexy man and many interruptions from her goofy dog.

Connect with Cecilia online!
www.cecilialane.com

Made in the USA
Monee, IL
22 April 2022

95198258R10198